Pecking
Order

Pecking Order

KEVIN McCOLLEY

HarperCollins*Publishers*

Library of Congress Cataloging-in-Publication Data
McColley, Kevin.
    Pecking order / Kevin McColley.
        p.   cm.
    Summary: Tom and his family experience many changes during the last year that their Minnesota farm is in operation.
    ISBN 0-06-023554-3. — ISBN 0-06-023555-1 (lib. bdg.)
    [1. Family problems—Fiction.   2. Farm life—Minnesota—Fiction.   3. Conduct of life—Fiction.   4. Minnesota—Fiction.]   I. Title.
PZ7.M13385Pe   1994   93-17768
[Fic]—dc20   CIP
                                                                              AC

1   2   3   4   5   6   7   8   9   10
❖
First Edition

This one is for my dad,
a former farmer, David McColley

Pecking Order

In the sweat of thy face shalt thou eat bread,
till thou return unto the ground;
for out of it wast thou taken:
for dust thou art,
and unto dust shalt thou return.
　　—Genesis 3:19

Hellfire and brimstone!
　　—The Reverend Ambrose Carstairs

CHAPTER ONE

I tell you what—if I had my choice, I'd be back on the farm. I kid you not. And I don't even like the farm. I can't *stand* it.

This farm I can't stand is in southern Minnesota, five miles south of Elder Falls. It's called the Morrell farm because Morrells have lived there ever since Adam wrote the Bible. Right before the Civil War, my great-great-great-grampa Justin Morrell homesteaded it. After he died, his son Theodore took it over, then Robert, then Grampa August, and finally Dad. During the Sioux uprising, Justin shot at Little Crow, the Dakota war chief, as he stood on the hill that's now part of the southern field. Theodore tracked down Cole Younger after Jesse James raided Northfield. Robert caught the flu in World War I and was left in a pile of dead flu victims at the Elder Falls train station,

3

where his wife, Greta, found him and nursed him back to health. Grampa August was a hero in World War II.

Dad never did anything. He didn't fight Indians or track down outlaws or get thrown in a corpse pile or *anything*. He never had any fun.

"Your dad was quiet," my friend Clint said. "And that can be good or bad."

But there's no such thing as a quiet Morrell—fire runs in our blood. Dad didn't end up quiet. If you can call what happened to him exciting, I guess you can say he lived up to the family tradition.

Two hundred years from now, people will climb into their Chevy rockets and blast into the sky. They'll look down and see this old beaten-up house, a barn, and a pasture next to a creek with a really good sledding hill along one side. "Yep," they'll say, "that's the Morrell farm." And it will be, it will always be, even though no Morrells will be living there. That's just the way that is.

I lived there with Jackey and Mom and Dad. We don't live there now. Not any of us. And that's just the way *that* is.

Since Dad raised cash crops for a living, he only kept enough livestock to be annoying. Not annoying to him, annoying to me. I had to feed and clean up after two hogs and a flock of chickens, and I was only twelve. Dad called them groceries on feet. I called them a pain in the butt.

One night a couple of springs ago, I was feeding the hogs. They smacked the feed around and spit half of it out and rutted through it and, well, made pigs out of themselves. My little brother, Jackey, was sitting behind me on a stack of hay bales.

"Those pigs are darn messy, Tom."

"Don't let Mom hear you cuss like that."

"What Mom don't know won't hurt her."

"Maybe I'll just tell her. Maybe I'll just make sure she knows."

"No you won't."

"Yes I will."

"Naw!"

I let the hogs rut awhile longer before I watered them. They were just as bad with their water as they were with their feed. They'd suck in a mouthful and let it dribble back out, carrying backwash with it. Then they drank the same water *again*. It made me sick just to watch them.

"Let's go, Jackey."

"I'll go when I want to."

Jackey was a stubborn little kid. He wouldn't do anything he didn't want to do. Shoot, he wouldn't do anything he *wanted* to do, if he knew you wanted him to do it, too. That's just the way he was.

"Well I'm leaving. You can stay if you want."

"I'm staying."

"Okay, but I have to turn the light off. And you know what happens to hogs in the dark."

He stared at me. "What?"

"They grow fangs. They eat people."

"They do not."

I shrugged. "Okay, don't believe me. See you later." I went to the door and shut off the light. "Maybe."

"Wait!" He barreled out like a Kmart shopper after the blue light special. "I decided I want to leave now, too."

I tell you what, that kid would fall for anything. If I had told him the Easter Bunny hops because he got the squirts from eating too much candy, he'd have believed me.

As we stepped outside, I grabbed his shoulder. I had something I wanted to try on him, and it would take some pretty delicate maneuvering.

"Do you want to play a game of Parcheesi?" I asked. Jackey liked Parcheesi.

"You mean now?"

"Why not?"

"We're not done."

"What do you mean?" I knew what he meant, of course.

"The chickens," Jackey said. "You forgot about the chickens."

"Oh, that's right." I slapped my forehead, just for

6

effect. "You remember the chickens better than I do." We headed off across the yard.

The wind was blowing warm from the south. The rich smells of blossoms and fresh-plowed earth whirled around our heads. The sun was red and orange and yellow on the horizon. It was setting later every night.

"Spring," Clint always said, "is when God says, 'What the heck? I'll give it another try.'"

"It's going to be damn warm tonight," I said as we crossed the yard.

"Don't let Mom hear you talk like that."

"What Mom don't know won't hurt her."

There were three parts to the Morrell chicken operation: the storage shed, where we kept the feed, tar, and chicken hooks; the coop, where the hens nested; and the brooder house, which held the new chicks. We waded through the shadows to the shed.

"I sure like chickens," Jackey said.

"I'm glad you do."

I poured a few handfuls of rolled oats in one ice-cream pail and filled another with cracked corn. Jackey grabbed the tar bucket, and we headed for the brooder house.

The brooder house was round—it had to be. Chicks pile up in corners and smother each other. The air inside was hot from the warming lamps and smelled of old feed, old sweat, and old chicken manure. We bought fifty white leghorns that year: thirty sexed female and twenty straight run, which means they can be any old sex. I scattered the rolled oats inside the cardboard wall that kept the chicks under the lamps. They went nuts. It looked like someone had dumped a boxful of peeping tennis balls on the floor.

"Keep your eyes open for pecked ones," I said.

Jackey never really did anything as far as chores go; he just followed me around. Dad said he was too little—too little my butt. I helped with the chickens when I was eight, and nobody was too little then. Dad just liked to spoil Jackey rotten.

"So you like chickens, huh?" I asked.

"I love chickens. Here comes a pecked one." He nabbed it.

"Good." I picked up the tar bucket. "From now on they're your job. Is that all right with you?"

"Sure!"

I rubbed the back of my neck, like I was worried he might get in trouble. "I don't know what Dad will say, though. He might think you're too little."

"I'm not too little."

"I know that, but Dad—"

"Don't worry about Dad. I can handle him." He held up the chick.

Am I smooth, or what? First I had to take care of the chickens, and then with a little fast talking

8

Jackey volunteered, and as long as Dad wanted to spoil him there was nothing he could do about it. I bet I've watched a ba-zillion spy movies, so I know what smooth is. I've seen spies catch villains and make all the beautiful women fall in love with them, without even messing up their hair, but they never once did anything as smooth as what I'd just done to Jackey.

The chick tried to scoot out of Jackey's hands, but he held its neck down gently with his thumb. "Is there a superhero who protects chickens?" he asked.

"I don't think so."

"Good. That's what I'll be when I grow up." The chick had a peck wound on its shoulder. I covered it with a dab of tar. If you don't cover a chick's wounds, the other chicks will kill it. They go crazy when they smell blood. All chickens do.

When we finished, we went outside. It was darker than it had been before. Everything looked like an old black-and-white movie.

"I just thought of something," Jackey said. "I can't feed the chickens." He leaned way over and dug at his crotch like a gold miner working away at the mother lode. Jackey could be pretty disgusting sometimes. Once I saw him blow a booger into his palm and shake the Reverend Carstairs' hand.

"What do you mean, you can't feed the chickens?"

"I'm too little to get the darn old feed bags down."

"Watch your mouth."

"You watch your mouth. You swear just as much as I do."

"I'm older."

"So?"

"What do you mean, so?" Little kids are so stupid. "So I can do what I want."

"I'll tell Mom and we'll just see about that, you big dummy."

You just can't argue with a stubborn little kid like Jackey. "Feed the chickens."

He took the pail from me and scattered the corn over the yard. What hens were there started pecking. The others came out of their roosts in the trees to join them.

"I'll feed them tonight, but I can't tomorrow," Jackey said. "I can't reach the bags."

He had me there. "I'll take the bags down. You just do the feeding." It looked like I'd get stuck with the chickens after all, or at least part of them.

By then, all the hens were out of the trees. We didn't keep roosters over the winter—if we had, they might have bred with the hens, and there's no way to tell a fresh fertilized egg from a fresh unfertilized one. Nothing's grosser than finding an embryo in your omelet.

"Look at 'em go!" Jackey said.

"Yeah." Big deal.

"I mean, just look at 'em!" Their white bodies squabbled around his feet. He looked like a picture I saw once of Jesus ascending through the clouds. "I sure like chickens."

Only the biggest hens were feeding. Whenever the smaller ones tried to jump in, they got pecked at until they ran away. They didn't get to eat until the bigger ones were done.

"Why do they pick on the little ones like that, Tom? Seems like the little ones never get to eat. Seems like they'll always stay little that way."

"It's called a pecking order."

He stared at me with this stupid expression on his face. I could tell he'd never heard of a pecking order before. He'd never heard of *anything* before. Jackey was an ignorant. It took so much time to teach him about the things he didn't know, I hardly had time to learn anything myself.

"It's like playing king of the hill," I said. "The big chickens are the kings and the others try to knock them off." I thought that was pretty good, coming off the top of my head like that.

"They're too little to knock them off. Why don't the big ones just let them eat?"

"If they did, the little ones would live long enough to have chicks. This way the strongest re-produce and the weaker die off. It's called propaga-tion of the species."

"Propa-who of the what?"

11

"Propagation of the species. Only the strong survive." Charles Darwin. We studied him in science. Darwin invented a thing called evolution. He thought it up while studying beagles.

"But if there's enough for everybody, why can't the weak survive, too?"

You just can't teach kids. "It's just the way things are."

He watched them. "Which chicken is the king of the hill?"

"That one." I pointed at a monster hen standing right in the middle of the feed. Her name was Cleo, and she was kind of a pet of mine. Cleo was bigger and whiter than the other hens. Somehow she looked more chicken than they did, almost chicken divine, almost chicken *holy*. If the Greeks had been chickens, she'd have looked like Helen or one of the other goddesses standing on the awards platform after winning the Olympics.

"She doesn't look so tough," Jackey said. "If I was a chicken, I could take her."

"If you were a chicken, you'd be so far down the pecking order, you'd never propagate."

He mulled it over for a while, then shrugged. There's a lesson in that. If you ever want to end an argument fast, use words the other person doesn't know. My teacher once charged me with shooting spitballs. I told her that her accusation was based entirely on circumcisional evidence. She looked at me like I had bugs crawling out of my ears. There are advantages to a big vocabulary.

One runt hen hadn't eaten yet. When she tried to, Cleo squawked and jabbed her shoulder. A little blood spot popped out, and when the other hens saw it, they started pecking her, too. She took off to hide in the trees.

"Mean old Cleo," Jackey muttered. "That poor little hen never gets enough to eat."

"She's at the bottom of the pecking order. She never will."

He braced his fists on his hips, the way he did when he got mad. "Pretty darn stupid."

"Hey—"

"I know. Watch my mouth. It's still pretty darn stupid." He screwed up his face like he thought he was thinking. "I know what I'm going to do."

"What?"

"Now that I'm in charge of the chickens, I'll put the little one in a pen by herself. I'll feed her and she'll get big and strong and I'll name her Chester."

"Chester is a boy's name."

"Chickens don't care what they're called, as long as they're called something. I'm going to put her in her own pen and call her Chester."

I shook my head. "If you do, then another hen'll get pushed down to the bottom of the pecking order.

Instead of having one skinny chicken, we'll have two."

"Oh." He was quiet for a long time.

I watched the chickens for as long as I could stand. "Let's go." We put the pails and tar away and headed across the yard. I scattered chickens with my feet as I went.

The moon shone down like God's flashlight. Mom and Dad were sitting on the porch. They liked to watch the sun set over the fields.

"Clean up before you come in," Mom called.

"All right." We walked to the back door.

"Maybe I can slip Chester some food once in a while when the other chickens aren't looking," Jackey said. "I can do that now that I'm in charge, can't I?"

"Sure." I held the door for him. "This is America. You can do anything you want."

CHAPTER TWO

The hallway running from the door to the kitchen smelled just as bad as the brooder house. On one side of it was a small bathroom. A stairwell going down to the basement was on the other.

We stripped off our boots and overalls. Jackey ducked into the bathroom ahead of me, but that didn't make any difference.

"Elders first." I yanked him out, then pushed by him to the sink.

"Hey!" He rolled up a bath towel and snapped the back of my neck. After I konked him a good one, he left me alone.

I scrubbed real good, way down into my pores, where the chicken manure odor settled. I always did that after chores—there's no surer way to say "I'm a hick" then to smell like one. When I finished, I walked to the porch.

15

Mom and Dad were watching the moon rise over Little Crow's field. A moth danced around the light fixture, banging its head against it like a fool. Dad was playing his guitar. He could pound out "Oh Susanna" like a pro.

Dad spent his whole life on the farm, except when he served in the Army. My uncle Eugene was in the Army, too. He got to fight in Vietnam and everything. He parachuted into the jungle and never came out again. Dad spent his whole enlistment in Georgia. Like I said, he never had any fun.

"Are you hungry?" Mom's green eyes glowed through the steam rising from her teacup. "I made some pies after work." Mom worked part-time at the Elder Falls Nursing Home.

"Sure," I said. "I'm always hungry." I tell you what, there was nothing better than Mom's pie.

I started for the kitchen, but she stopped me. "I'll get it." She stood and went inside.

Mom's name was Abby. She looked like that woman on TV who does the coffee commercials, except her nose was kind of small and she had wrinkles around her eyes. They were from laughing, so that wasn't so bad.

While we waited, Dad strummed softly and I watched the night come on. The moth banged its head a good one on the light and had to rest on the porch screen to compose itself.

16

"All the planting's done." Dad's voice was as rich and deep as a shout in a well. It was the kind of voice a mountain would have.

"How'd it go?" I didn't really care how it went—I was just being polite. All I cared about was that it was over. I wouldn't have to help with it anymore.

"Fine. The soil's black. Smells black, too. I like that in the spring." He studied the calluses on his palms. Next to Ello Tohrey, our neighbor, Dad had the biggest hands in the world. He could palm a water buffalo, no lie.

Mom came back with the pie and two glasses of milk. I dug in. Dad rested his guitar against the wall, then stretched, his fingers trembling as they clawed the air. "Planting sure takes a hell of a lot out of you," he said.

Mom slapped his arm. "Don't swear in front of the boys, honey." Mom was from Georgia—that's where she met Dad. She had this funny Southern accent, as if she gargled with thirty-weight motor oil every morning. "What would your mother say?"

"My mother wouldn't care."

"Then what about Reverend Carstairs?"

"I know what he'd say," I broke in. "Hellfire and brimstone!" Me and Dad both laughed.

Mom clicked her tongue. "For goodness' sake, John, now you've got the boys doing it."

Mom loved Jesus. I don't mean that in a bad way,

17

like she was a Bible thumper or something, I just mean that she liked to go to church and pray and sing anthems—a Southern Baptist Southern Belle, that's what Dad called her. Unless she was doing farmwork she was always clean, and she was always polite, and she never, ever took the Lord's name in vain. We didn't either. Not in front of her, anyway.

Religionwise, Mom was pretty close to normal, except for once when her sister, Maggie, died in a car wreck. She hid out for three days in an empty room upstairs and did nothing but pray, read her Bible, and tell everyone how evil they were. The monks in the dark ages used to do that when times got tough. They called monasteries abbeys back then. Maybe that's where Mom got her name.

"Where are you, John, Jr.?" she called into the house.

"Comin'," Jackey hollered back.

"If you want pie, you better come now."

"I said I'm comin'!" Feet tramped over the kitchen linoleum. Jackey bolted onto the porch and grabbed the last piece of pie.

"I got a joke for you, Dad," he said.

"Oh?"

"What's black and white and red all over?"

Dad mulled about it for a while. I don't know why. Jackey told him the same joke not a week before.

"I give up."

18

"A skunk with diaper rash!"

Dad nearly fell out of his chair. Even Mom giggled. How a joke they'd heard only a week before could be so hilarious the second time around is beyond me. It wasn't even funny the first time.

When they finally calmed down enough for the red to drain from their faces, Jackey spoke up again. "Guess what, Dad."

"What?"

"Tom put me in charge of the chickens tonight."

"He did?" Dad's eyes flashed at me. He didn't like me delegating chores.

"He's following me around during chores anyway," I griped. "He might as well do something."

"That's for me to decide."

"What else does he do? Shoot, when I was eight I was working around here."

"That was different."

"How was that different?"

"It just was."

Jackey wolfed down half his pie in two bites. He ate like the hogs. I turned my head when he drank his milk.

"I waffa doof if," he said.

"Don't speak with your mouth full."

He swallowed. "I wanna do it."

"I don't know," Mom said. "It seems to me boys should be boys for as long as they can."

I glared at her. "You didn't say that when Dad started me on the chickens."

"You were older."

"I was eight!"

"You were born older."

I shut up. I didn't know how to argue when she threw stuff like that at me.

Dad looked at Jackey. "Are you sure you want to do this?"

"Yeah."

"All right, as long as you know you don't have to." He finished his pie.

Well, la-di-da. I guess we all know now who the favorite in *this* family was.

Dad stood up and stretched again. "I'm going to bed."

"Already?"

"Tomorrow we have to get up early." He stared at me with a look that said, "I'm going to ruin your weekend and you're going to like it."

"Aw, Dad! Saturdays are the only day I get to sleep in late."

"Ello Tohrey's working on his tractor in the morning."

"What help could I be to him?"

"That's not the point. The point is he'll teach you how to be a mechanic."

"But Dad—"

20

"How do you expect to run a farm if you can't make simple tractor repairs?"

Whoever said anything about running a farm? "Can't we do it in the afternoon?"

"Do you have something better to do in the morning?"

I thought about lying but decided not to. I lie to other people, at least a few juicy ones a couple times a week, but me and Dad never lied to each other. "No."

"Good. Then I'll see you bright and early."

"Damn it." I swore before I knew I had. Cuss words are greasy. They slip out when you least expect them to.

Mom looked at me as if I'd stuck my fork in the belly of a newborn puppy. "You watch your mouth. I've a good mind to wash it out with soap."

I was mad enough to swear again, but I didn't. The satisfaction of profanity doesn't make up for the agony of sucking on a bar of Ivory. I know.

Dad stepped behind Mom and kissed her neck. He whispered something I couldn't hear. She smiled. Mom watched him go into the house, then looked at me.

"It won't be so bad," she said.

"Yeah, right." How would she know? She didn't know anything. Nobody knew anything.

"I'll go," Jackey said. "I like Mr. Tohrey."

21

There was an idea. "Yeah, why can't he go instead?"

"Because your father wants you to. He's proud of you and wants to show you off."

I shrugged. More of that stuff I didn't know how to argue with.

"Isn't he proud of me?" Jackey asked.

"Of course he is," Mom said. "You can go, too."

"Good." Jackey smiled. Pie dough was stuck to his teeth. Sometimes he made me want to puke.

Mom ran her fingers through her long red hair—auburn, she called it. She glanced at the bedroom door where Dad had gone and forced a yawn. Any fool could see she wasn't tired.

"I'm going to turn in, too," she said. "Make sure all the lights are off before you go to bed, okay?"

"Okay."

"And not too late, you hear?"

"Yeah."

"Good night, guys." She stood, smiled, and kissed us both, then yawned and went in the house.

Who was she trying to kid? That might work on Jackey, but not on me. *I* knew what they were up to. I didn't just fall off the turnip truck, you know.

"So you wanna watch TV?" Jackey asked.

"For a little while." We went inside. Jackey found a program about a talking dog that saves the world. It only had one pretty woman and she never even had

22

the decency to wear a bikini. Fifteen minutes into it, I'd had as much as I could stand. I went for a walk. I like walks.

When I got back, the dog thing was over. Jackey was watching a show about a private investigator. I shut the TV off.

"What did you do that for?"

"It's bedtime."

"Already? No!" He grabbed my leg. "Mom and Dad won't let me stay up by myself. If you go to bed, then I have to."

"Tough."

"Come on, Tom. Just a little while?"

"No." I dragged him like a ball and chain to the porch. I waited until the moth made a big run at the fixture before I shut the light off. It must have thought the world exploded. I turned off the lights in the living room and headed for the stairs.

"Please, Tom?"

"No."

"Why?"

"Because I have to get up early." And if I was going to be miserable in the morning, Jackey was going to be miserable that night. I shook him loose, then half led and half dragged him up the stairs.

He sat on his bed and glared at me. Boy, if looks could kill. "Darn old bully. You never let me have any fun."

I lay down. "Shut up."

"Make me."

"If you're not careful, I will."

"I'm not even tired. How am I supposed to sleep when I'm not even tired? You answer me that, you big—"

"I said shut up." I'd heard as much out of him as I was going to. I wanted to sulk, and I couldn't get any good sulking done listening to that big baby whine. Finally he shut off the light and lay down.

I didn't care what Dad said. There was no *way* I was going to end up stuck on a farm. I was going to the city. I was going to get away from the fields and away from the tractors and away from the stinking manure. The closest thing to manure I'd ever see would be dog poop on the sidewalk, and I could step *around* that.

My eyelids grew heavy faster than I thought they would. I bet Jackey was still pouting when I fell asleep.

CHAPTER THREE

Bright and early on the Morrell farm meant just that—bright and early. It meant sun-rising, rooster-crowing, what-in-God's-name-am-I-doing-up? early.

"Just be glad you don't live on a dairy farm," Dad told me at breakfast. "You'd have been up hours ago."

"I know, I know." My head almost dropped into my cereal bowl. "So what's the matter with the Tohrey tractor?" I needed to talk about something to stay awake. Anything. Even tractors.

"Not much. He wanted to change the plugs and look at the points last night, but I asked him to wait until this morning."

"Why?"

"So you could help."

"You mean I got up this early for something that could have been done last night?"

"Yep."

25

"Gee, thanks." I hoped he noticed the sarcasm in my voice.

I finished my cereal, then went outside to do the chores. The air was still cool enough to drive some of the sleep away.

When I finished with the hogs, I went to the shed and filled the feed pails. I was about to yawn my way over to the brooder house when I remembered Jackey.

Whoa, now wait just a minute. Feeding the chickens was *his* job. It'd been agreed on the whole way around, and there was no way I was going to do it for him. I set the pails down and left.

Cleo was searching for bugs by the coop. "You're top banana and you know it, don't you?" I asked her. She clucked once and stretched out her neck. I scratched her.

It's a funny feeling, scratching a chicken. With the feathers and quills, it's soft and hard at the same time. A chicken must feel the same way a pioneer shot full of Indian arrows must have felt. I'd hate to be a chicken. I'd always be shouting to circle the wagons.

Chester cowered under one corner of the storage shed, watching us. When I stepped toward her, she ducked out of sight. Jeez, what a way to live. I headed for the house.

Just as I turned the corner of the coop, Jackey

26

came flying around it. He scowled at me the same way Superman would right after Lex Luthor shoved kryptonite in his underwear.

"Why didn't you wake me?"

"Why should I have?"

"You knew I wanted to come along."

"So?" What was the big deal about watching me fix a tractor? *I* didn't even want to watch me fix a tractor.

"You didn't feed the chickens, did you?" he asked.

"No, but I filled the pails."

"How's Chester?"

"I didn't look." I did, but I didn't care.

"Dad's in the truck. He says we're leaving as soon as the chores are done."

"Then you better get a move on." He darted around the corner. I shuffled to the driveway where the pickup waited.

"Now I want you to pay close attention to every-thing Ello does," Dad said as I climbed in beside him. "That man can tune an engine better by ear than any mechanic with a computer can."

"Yeah."

"And if you have any questions, ask him."

"I will." But I didn't think I'd have any.

Jackey ran across the yard and hopped in beside me. The sun had dried the dew off the driveway gravel enough for us to kick up a dust plume as we left.

Ello Tohrey was a bear. That's the only way I could describe him. A bear. He was built like a bear and he walked like a bear, and when he spoke, he growled deep in his throat like one. A bear came down from the north woods, shaved himself, and bought a farm.

"How ya doin', Jack?" Ello lumbered from the house to the truck. Dad was Jack to everyone except me and Mom and Jackey.

"Can't complain."

"And you brought the boys, Pete and repeat. How ya doin', Doc?" Ello called every kid Doc. As I stepped out of the cab, he punched my arm. I tried to punch him back, but he blocked my fist and punched me again. That's the way he greeted me. With bruises.

"By God," he growled, "I can still take you. Don't forget that, Doc." Ello always pronounced "God" "Gud." I think he was trying to swear and slip one over on the Almighty at the same time.

"The Lord sees all," the Reverend Carstairs said. "He knows our very hearts."

"If the Lord sees all, then we're all in trouble," Clint always said. "Especially Reverend Carstairs."

While I tried to get some circulation back in my arm, Ello scanned the yard, as if he was searching for a moose to devour. "Where's the other one? I thought you brought a great big guy with you. Scared the life out of me when he stepped out of the truck."

"Right here, Mr. Tohrey." Jackey was hiding behind the cab door. Kids were always shy around Ello. When I was a kid, I was the same way.

"Well, there you are! Good God, boy, you're getting to be a monster. Put 'er there." Ello's hand swallowed Jackey's. He shook it so hard, it seemed that Jackey's arm would rip off and fly across the yard. A terrified look popped out of Jackey's face; then Ello laughed and let go. Jackey smiled and held his hand out again. He wanted more.

Nobody but Ello Tohrey could do that. I'd seen it a thousand times, with bruises on arms and hands shook off and loud, wet raspberries on babies' faces. If anyone else tried it, the kids would cry. With Ello, they laughed. I couldn't figure it out.

"You know, Doc," Ello said to Jackey, "I've been having trouble catching that black-and-yellow cat." He pointed toward the house. The cat's head popped up as if it knew what Ello was talking about. "It seems that you're the only one around here who can catch cats. Put him in the barn and I have a dollar for ya."

Jackey pushed up his sleeves. "No problem, Mr. Tohrey." He hid behind a tree, then tiptoed across the yard. The cat darted around the house. Jackey took off after it like a fat-farm escapee chasing an ice-cream truck.

29

"So you've come to learn how to work on a tractor, huh, Doc?" Ello led us toward the utility shed.

"I guess so." I tried to make it clear I wasn't enjoying myself. It was the only rebellion I had.

"I ain't got much to show ya," Ello said. "Just working on the plugs and points."

"It's a start," Dad answered for me.

"Yeah, and good God, it's about time you started." Ello punched me again, then slid the shed door open. The sunlight fell inside on a Minneapolis-Moline tractor so old it had caveman paintings on the seat. Ello walked over to the workbench, then came back with a ratchet hidden somewhere in his hand.

"Why do you keep this piece of junk?" I asked.

Ello looked at me like I'd just puked in his Froot Loops. "Don't call Molly junk. She's a classic." He threatened me with the ratchet before he started pulling the spark plug wires.

"You should get a new Steiger," I said. "George Shade has one. It's air-conditioned with a stereo and everything."

Ello grunted. "Why would I want a tractor like that?"

"It's a lot bigger than Molly. In one day you'd get as much done as four days on her."

"And what would I do with all that free time? I'd sit on my butt in the cafe with the other Steiger owners, getting fat. No thanks." He spun the ratchet. It clicked like a pissed-off cricket.

"George does a lot more than sit on his butt," I said. "He's one of the richest farmers in the county." He was so rich you couldn't really call him a farmer. He hired people to do his farming for him.

Ello looked at Dad and Dad looked at Ello and they both shook their heads. "I don't want money if it means getting it the way he does," Ello muttered.

"Why? How's he get it?"

"You don't want to hear about that, Doc." Ello returned to work, muttering.

The neat thing about Ello is that while he worked, he thought and talked, and he always talked about what he was thinking. "By God, you know what George is doing, don't you, Jack?"

"I know," Dad said.

Ello attacked the spark plugs the same way a dentist attacks a cavity. "It's a crime, the way he takes advantage of government subsidies. It's more than a crime. It's a sin."

I shrugged. "Seems to me if you can get government money, you should take it. That's the smart thing to do."

Ello shook his head. "Doc, there's good smart and there's bad smart, and what George Shade does isn't good smart." He pointed the ratchet at my chest. "It's not just a sin against the government, it's a sin against us. It's a sin against you."

"George has never done anything to me."

"He hasn't? He plants the cheapest corn he can

31

find, the crap that hardly germinates, then gets compensation on the amount his yield is below the county average. Not only does he get money he doesn't deserve, but he drives down the average and makes the rest of us look like we're overproducing, so our payments go down. That's food out of your mouth."

"Still—"

"Still nothing. George Shade is more crooked than a turd out of a shivering dog. Don't you talk to me about George Shade."

I watched him work. Dad stood by the door, gazing at the fields.

"George Shade, by God." Ello set his ratchet down. I guess *I* couldn't talk about George, but *he* sure could. "Him and his Steigers and his big new buildings and all the land he's buying up. I hope he keeps spending his money. I hope he enjoys it while he can."

"Why?"

"Because what goes around comes around."

Dad laughed a laugh without any humor in it at all. "Then we should have a fortune coming. We're in debt up to our eyeballs."

"You talk like you're ashamed," Ello said.

Dad turned around. "Aren't you?"

"We have nothing to be ashamed of."

"What about the debt we can't pay?"

"That's not our fault. That's 1983's fault."

In 1983, the government started a program to decrease overproduction by paying farmers if they let their land lie fallow. Nearly half of all farmland was set aside. The same year a drought dropped production. You'd think that with such a low supply and such a high demand, prices would go through the roof. They didn't. The cartels shipped in grain from overseas to keep them down.

The farmers had low production *and* low prices. Everybody but the cartels lost money, and tens of thousands of farmers went under. Dad and Ello almost did. Both had been paying for it ever since.

"We're just poor country people," Dad said.

Ello spun his ratchet. "As long as we have the land, we're not poor."

"I don't have the land. The creditors do."

"As long as you're pouring your own blood and sweat into the land, it's yours."

"That's not what they say."

"Who, the banks? Banks don't know what blood and sweat are."

"I'm not talking just about the banks. Half my loans are with the Farmers Home Administration."

"It doesn't know what blood and sweat are, either."

"It should. It's sucked enough out of me to be able to recognize them."

Ello turned from the tractor. "You sound like you're ready to quit."

"I'd never quit," Dad said, "you know that. With a good year, everything will be fine." He sighed. "It's not supposed to be a good year."

"You don't know that."

"The forecasters are predicting drought."

"What do forecasters know?" Ello glared at me. "Are you learning anything?"

"How can I? You spend more time yapping than you do working."

"By God, I oughta . . ." He tensed up to punch me again, then lowered his fist. "Don't forget, Doc, I still can take you." He went back to work.

The sun was higher now. Dad's shadow lay across the floor as dead and still as a murdered ghost. The loans worried him. So did the weather. When I thought about them long enough, I guess they worried me, too, not so much because of what they might do to the farm as what they might do to Dad. I guess it was really the same thing.

I lied to Ello. I was learning a lot.

Ello showed me how to work the wires and set the spacing on the plugs and how to file the corrosion off the points. He told me how everything worked, from the points to the rotor to the plugs. When we finished, he started her up. Old Molly purred like a fat, happy kitten. "See if George Shade can do that to his Steiger." He laughed.

I laughed, too. I had to. I got off without touching the thing.

Just as Ello turned the engine off, Jackey marched through the door. "I caught the cat, Mr. Tohrey."

Ello climbed down and rubbed his chin. "I guess I owe you a dollar."

"Yep."

Ello dug into his pocket and handed Jackey a bill. His dirty fingers left a grease smear across Washington's face.

"The barn's full of holes, Mr. Tohrey. That cat's just gonna get away again."

"Then you'll have to catch him the next time you're here."

"Guess so." Jackey studied the bill, then shoved it into his pocket. "But you'll owe me another dollar."

"You sound like a banker." Ello laughed again.

"Let's go, boys," Dad said. "We have work to do at home."

"Thanks, Ello," I said on the way out. I didn't mean about the tractor; I didn't *care* about the tractor. I'm not sure what I meant.

"Anytime, Doc." He farewell punched me. When I tried to hit him back, he punched me again. I'd be lucky to get home still able to bend my arm. After Ello shook Jackey's hand, the three of us headed for the truck.

"Just a sec, Jack," Ello called, "let me talk to you.

35

You boys go on ahead." Dad walked back to the shed; me and Jackey to the pickup. Ello stood with one hand on Dad's shoulder. They both had their heads down. Ello said something I couldn't hear. I wondered what it was.

A door slammed and Kelly came out of the house. Ello and his wife, Lois, only had one kid, Kelly. Me and her were in the same class at school. Kelly's hair was the color of shadows under a tree, and she had these really bright brown eyes. She could beat me at almost everything. She was faster than me, and meaner than me, and she was even stronger than me. She was that way with just about everybody I knew. Kelly was a pretty neat guy, for a girl.

"Hey," she said.

"Hey." We said our heys all around.

"You guys coming over this afternoon?"

"It depends on what the old man has us doing." Dad was always the old man when he wasn't around. Mom was always the old lady.

"What would he have you doing?"

"Oh, I don't know. Farmwork, I guess." I almost hoped Dad would have us do something. I knew why Kelly wanted us to come over.

"Well, stop by the maple tree down in First Woods," she said. "We'll hold the world wrestling championships. It'll only take a few minutes." She grinned.

Every few weeks, Kelly wanted to hold the world wrestling championships at First Woods, the woods that divided our properties. That meant that every few weeks I got the snot beat out of me. Kelly worked in dirty fighting the same way Michelangelo worked in marble.

"I don't know," I said. "Can't we do something else?"

"I wanna wrestle," Jackey said. He would. She didn't do to him the things she did to me.

"Chicken," Kelly said to me.

"I am not."

"Chicken," Jackey repeated. "Bawk, bawk, bawk!"

"Shut up." I konked him. "Listen, can't we do something that uses our brains? How about a game of checkers?"

"Okay." She sneered. "I'll beat you at that, too."

I kind of chuckled, the way a person does when he knows he's superior. "How could you beat me in something that takes brains? You're just an idiot girl." Everybody knows girls are dumber than guys. That's why they're girls. Ask Charlie Darwin. It's genetics.

Kelly's arms dropped to her sides. She took two steps toward me. Her fists clenched. "Take that back."

"Take what back?" The idiot remark had slipped out so easily, I didn't realize I'd said anything.

"You know what." She tried to scratch my face, but I grabbed her wrists before she had a chance. I figured as long as I had her like that, I was all right. That was my first mistake.

Kelly whipped her hands out to the sides. As soon as my arms were clear, she butted me in the stomach with the top of her head.

My second mistake was to react to the pain. When I doubled over, she brought her head up and caught me under the chin. Cartoons don't lie. You really do see stars and little birdies.

You'd think she'd be satisfied with that. She wasn't.

"He must be dead." Jackey's voice was the first thing I heard when I came around. "No one could take that and just *lie* there." I didn't know what he was talking about, but then this feeling started. At first a feeling was all it was, my brain was so joggled up, but then it turned into a cold hollow pain, as if someone were scraping my insides out with a frosty spoon. When I opened my eyes, I saw it wasn't a spoon at all. I wished it had been. Kelly was digging away at my crotch with her nice, sharp fingernails. All ten of them.

You can probably guess what I did. I curled up like a worm around a fishhook.

"Take that back!" she demanded.

"I do, I do. I take it all back, every single word!"

"Are you sorry?"

"Oh yes, yes, you wouldn't believe how sorry I am. I didn't mean it, I never meant it, especially about you, just please, please, let go of my balls!"

After a little more begging, she did. I lay there, coughing and rolling. Kelly stood over me and waited until I could climb, gasping, to my feet.

"Don't ever say that again," she said.

"I won't." I *still* couldn't remember what I said.

"Are we friends?" she asked.

"Sure."

"Good. Sorry about your balls." She held out her hand and waited until I could hold out mine. We shook.

Well, what was I supposed to do? You think I wanted her as an *enemy*?

Dad came back before I could fully straighten up. "What happened to you?"

"He has a stomachache," Kelly said.

"Yeah." I wasn't about to disagree with her.

"Well, have your stomachache in the truck. We have to go."

As we headed down the driveway, Kelly smiled and waved. When we drove by the shed, Ello smiled and waved, too. Dad turned onto the road toward our house.

"I want you two to get the planter and tractor cleaned up when we get home," Dad said.

"Won't that take most of the afternoon?" I tried to hold my insides in as nonchalantly as I could.

"I don't care if it does. I don't want to hear any griping."

Griping? I was thanking God. Even farmwork would be better than going through another ball gouging. "What did you and Ello talk about?" I asked.

"Nothing." Dad kept his eyes on the road.

"It must have been something."

"Nothing important."

"A secret?" Jackey asked.

"Yeah," Dad said, "a secret."

I didn't say anything more. Dad and Jackey didn't either.

I didn't like that secret business one bit. It's one thing to have a secret, but it's another thing to have one kept from you. What good is a secret you don't know?

CHAPTER FOUR

Sunday morning meant ties, suits, and polished shoes. It meant Mom in a dress, the only time during the week she wore one. It meant the church growing hotter and hotter, until sweat rained down like the Holy Spirit on Pentecost. Sometimes I hated Sunday mornings.

We went to the Seat of Mercy Baptist church in Elder Falls. We used to go to the Ascension United Methodist church, but Mom insisted we change. She said she was born a Baptist and she'd die as one.

"Did you do your Sunday-school lesson, John, Jr.?" Mom asked on the drive in.

"Yeah." Big deal. All he had to do for his lesson was color pictures of the apostles. He gave Peter a green beard.

"How about you, Tom?"

41

"Of course."

She glanced over the back of her seat. "Then what are you doing now?"

"Reviewing." I didn't look up. I still had three questions to write out answers for.

Miss Spinner, my Sunday-school teacher, always gave the longest, hardest lessons. Once I had to read *two whole Bible chapters* and answer *ten questions*! I kept waiting for her to tell me to learn Hebrew and read the entire Bible's original text. I kept waiting for her to tell me to get inspired by God and write a new one.

The Elder Falls water tower floated above the town like a blue mushroom cloud signaling the Apocalypse the Reverend wass always yapping about. I gave up on the lesson when we reached city limits. There just wasn't time. Besides, it dealt with the miracle at Cana, when Jesus turned water to wine. That's always confused me. Why did he waste a perfectly good miracle on wine jugs? Why didn't he heal someone? Why didn't he heal me? My balls still ached.

"Let's be prayerful, class," Miss Spinner said. She always said that just when she thought we were about to have a good time. She pushed up her glasses. She wore black cat-eyes at least a ba-zillion years old—she probably got them way back when she was only eighty. They magnified her cheeks, and through their lenses every wrinkle was a sea trough, every downy hair a strand of gray seaweed tossing on a prune-faced ocean.

There were four of us in the class: me and Jeff and Clint and Marietta Carstairs. Marietta was the Reverend's granddaughter. She always sat by herself. She was too holy to sit with the rest of us. She might get *tainted*.

Us guys didn't mind. Marietta looked a lot like Miss Spinner.

"Why did Jesus turn the water to wine?" Miss Spinner stuck a hand-drawn picture of Jesus sitting next to three wine jugs on her Velcro board. From the way he was sprawled out, Jesus looked like he had drunk the three jugs dry himself.

"To symbolize the Holy Spirit's outpouring," Marietta said.

"Very good, Marietta." Marietta always answered the questions. She always knew the correct answers, the *doctrinal* answers. She got them from her grampa. The rest of us hated her.

"Miss Spinner," Clint asked, "isn't drinking alcohol a sin?" Clint always knew the correct responses to Marietta's doctrinal answers. He was a religious rebel and the smartest guy I knew. When he and Miss Spinner got going, it was like watching a boxing match.

"Of course it is," Miss Spinner said. "Alcohol is evil." A jab.

43

"If alcohol is evil and we're not supposed to drink it, why did Jesus perform a miracle to make some?" Clint throws a hard left hook to the body!

"Biblical wine was not the same as modern wine. It was more like grape juice." Another jab, and a pretty feeble one at that.

"*More* like? Are you saying it was somewhere between wine and grape juice? Are you saying it still had alcohol in it, just not as much as wine? And if it still had alcohol in it, and alcohol is evil, why did Jesus make it?" A roundhouse right to the forehead puts Miss Spinner on the ropes! Her mouthpiece has popped out!

"I'm saying it was grape juice. When the Bible says wine, it really means grape juice." Miss Spinner's right eye is swollen shut! Clint is pummeling her at will!

"Then when Jesus talked about putting new wine into old wineskins, what made the old wineskins burst? If the wine wasn't fermenting because it stayed grape juice, where did the pressure come from to burst them?" Clint throws a hard combination to the head! Miss Spinner is reeling!

Miss Spinner sighed. "Be quiet, Clint." *She's down!* The referee is starting the count!

"But—"

"I said be quiet, Clint."

"But—"

"I don't know, all right?" KNOCKOUT! Miss Spinner's out cold! Clint is still the undefeated heavyweight champion of the church! "Ask Reverend Carstairs."

"I already asked Mr. Carstairs—"

"Reverend," Marietta interrupted. "His name is the Reverend Ambrose Carstairs. *Not* Mr." She looked down her nose at Clint. She had enough nose left over to look down the rest of it at me and Jeff. Clint always called the Reverend Carstairs "mister" because he knew how mad calling him that made Marietta. He liked to make her mad. We all did.

Miss Spinner was about to put a picture of a hunchbacked Mary on her board when the bell rang, signaling the end of Sunday school. "Now class," she said, "don't forget to read—"

But that was all me, Jeff, and Clint heard. We were out the door before she had a chance to give us next week's lesson. We were every week. We planned it that way. Not that it mattered. Sometime during the week, Marietta always cornered us at school and made sure we knew. I don't know if she did that because she liked Sunday-school lessons or because she liked us not liking Sunday-school lessons. Either way she did it. Either way we hated her.

"You guys gonna sit up front?" Jeff looked up at us when we reached the foyer. He was at least a mile shorter than me and Clint.

"I know why you want to sit up front," Clint said. "You want to stare at Mrs. Kramer." Mrs. Kramer sang soprano with Mom in the choir. Her husband, Roger, was one of the three officers on the Elder Falls police force. He used to be an athlete, but he wasn't anymore. All those free doughnuts at the Honeybee Cafe were building up around his middle. Nothing built up around Mrs. Kramer's middle. She was built up a little higher.

I once asked Mom if she could describe Mrs. Kramer in one word. She said, "Ample. Mrs. Kramer is ample." I looked up "ample" in the dictionary. It means "enough to satisfy." That was Mrs. Kramer all over.

"My old man won't let me sit with you guys," I said. "Not after last week." During the prayer the week before, Clint had started a burping contest. Clint was a world-class burper. "Tell me what Mrs. Kramer is wearing when the service is over." From our pew, we couldn't see the choir.

"I bet it's that low-cut blue dress," Clint said.

"I hope so." Jeff giggled.

They were so excited, they pretty near sprinted up the aisle, then sat down not more than three feet from where Mrs. Kramer would sit in all her glory when the choir came in. I sure hoped Dad would get over that burping thing soon. Warm weather was coming, and Mrs. Kramer always dressed appropriately.

46

Dad came into the foyer, dragging Jackey behind him. Jackey had one finger under his collar, pulling at the snugness of his tie. He didn't like ties. He screwed his face up like he'd just eaten a big plate of raw liver à la mode.

"How was Sunday school?" Dad asked.

"Same as always." We didn't go into the sanctuary. We never did until the very last minute. Dad didn't like spending any more time in there than he had to.

"Hi, Jack." Joe Tristam came over and shook Dad's hand. Behind him came Mary, his wife. She was hanging on to their son's fist. His name was Muddle-Head.

That wasn't his real name. His real name was Merle. Everyone called him Muddle-Head when no parents were around.

"Awfully dry for this early in the year, isn't it?" Joe asked.

"Sure is," Dad answered.

"Gyaah," Muddle-Head said. He had his free fist shoved in his mouth. It was slimy with drool.

"Weather this dry is good for pheasants, though," Joe said, ignoring Muddle-Head. "Are you going to blast some birds with me this year?" The Tristams lived down the road from us.

"We'll have to see." Joe made Dad uncomfortable. That whole family made me uncomfortable. Mary was weird because she spent all her time apologizing

47

for Muddle-Head. Joe was weird because he loved to shoot things, and you never knew what he was going to shoot next. Or who. Once, when he'd had a few too many beers, he loaded up and blasted the mailman. He knocked his hat off.

And then, of course, there was Muddle-Head. He was like eighteen years old, but he acted like he was two. He had these little piggy eyes you could hardly see because of skinfolds over them. Everyone said he had Down syndrome. I thought he was just plain goofy.

Muddle-Head spent all his time wandering around the neighborhood. Shoot, sometimes it wasn't just the neighborhood but the whole county—more than once the sheriff picked him up in Elder Falls and had to drive him home. Sometimes he came right in our yard, or in the house even, and he'd take stuff and walk away with it. No lie. Mom said he didn't know better.

Didn't know better, my butt. He was a lot smarter than he let himself on to be. There was nothing wrong with Muddle-Head that a good slap to the side of the face wouldn't have cured. That's what I always thought, anyway. I wondered if anyone had tried it.

Dad went in the sanctuary first, then me, then Jackey. Mrs. Hemmer, the church organist, began playing just as we reached our pew.

"Confucius say," Clint always said, "man who go

to bathroom in church sit in his own pew." Clint was pretty cool.

Jackey started fidgeting as soon as we sat down. "These seats are so darn hard," he whispered.

"Don't swear in church," I whispered back.

"Why not? The Reverend says hell and damn all the time. If he can swear, I can."

"That's different."

"How is it different?"

What a dumb kid. "It's—"

Dad cleared his throat. I shut up. I can take a hint.

Mrs. Hemmer stopped playing, cranked on the volume knob, and began the first hymn. I opened the hymnal and held it so Jackey could see. The hymn was "Here I Raise Mine Ebenezer."

Don't ask me. I don't know either.

Mrs. Hemmer was half deaf. She always played the opening hymn loud. Once last winter, during "Rock of Ages," the organ vibrated the snow off the roof and buried Wally, the janitor, while he was shoveling the walk. Nobody heard him swearing until the prayer began. The ushers had to dig him out.

There was one good one thing about her playing loud, though—she covered up the old people's voices. Old people sing worse than anyone else in the world, and our church was packed with them. Their voices reminded me of a mole that snuck into our basement once. I was about to smack it a good one with a two-by-four when it looked at me and screamed. Jesus Criminey, you've never heard such a godawful sound in your life. It scared me so bad I wet my pants. That's what the Almighty must do when old people sing.

Beneath all the mole screams, Dad's deep bass voice rolled like distant thunder. Dad never sang loud in church. He did in the fields, but never in church. I think he felt trapped worshipping indoors. When you work outside a lot, you get that way.

When the hymn ended, the Reverend stepped to the pulpit. Ambrose Carstairs was the oldest old fart you ever saw. There wasn't a young thing on him. His ears were old and his nose was old and the silver hair that fringed his mottled old scalp was old. He had old watery eyes that somehow I knew never saw what he was looking at. The Reverend only saw what he wanted to see.

"Praise the Lord," the Reverend said.

"Praise the Lord," a few people mumbled back.

"I SAID PRAISE THE LORD!"

"PRAISE THE LORD!" If he couldn't get them there any other way, the Reverend could always shout people into the Spirit.

The Reverend read the announcements. Instead of listening, I got down to work on my bulletin, doodling in the margins rockets taking off and cities being eaten by monsters. When I finished, the Reverend was still only in the middle of the prayer, so I filled in all the e's and o's and p's in the typeset. That took up all the time until the choir anthem, when I listened to Mom singing.

Jeez, she had a nice voice. You'd think that between her and Dad I would have gotten a little musical talent, but no way. My voice sounds like a gassy toad.

After the anthem came the sermon.

You should have seen Clint impersonate the Reverend preaching. After gym class, he stood on a bench in his jockstrap and made his face wrinkled. I'm not sure how he did it, but he did, and then he started sermonizing.

"Woe unto you, idolaters! Woe unto all you who blaspheme the Lord's name. Muslims, Buddhists, Hindus, Catholics, Jews, do you want to know what awaits you? Hellfire and brimstone!" It was the funniest thing you ever saw.

The Reverend stood in the pulpit, waving his arms like he was beating off Beelzebub. The congregation moaned as if their flesh was already cooking off their bones. Not that they were afraid of hell—they didn't need to be. They were saved. They were pitying all the poor heathen that would burn. That's one thing our church was full of. Pity.

The Reverend got so excited he knocked the

51

microphone off its stand. As it flip-flopped through the air, thunder like God's wrath echoed over the loudspeakers. When it plopped into Mrs. O'Reilly's lap, the thunder gave way to the scratchy whistle of polyester against polyester. Mrs. O'Reilly looked down at the microphone, then back up at the Reverend. She didn't know what to do.

The Reverend Carstairs knew what to do. Before the congregation had time to break from its agony, he was on the floor chasing down the microphone like the devil after a lost soul. When his hand plunged into Mrs. O'Reilly's lap, her arms flew up in the air.

"EEEOWWWEEEEK!" Mrs. O'Reilly raised a cry unto the Lord.

"Woe unto you!" the Reverend shouted at her. Mrs. O'Reilly had once been Catholic, and I think the Reverend suspected her of being a Roman spy sent to infiltrate and destroy the house of the one true God. She fainted dead away. Old Mrs. Matthews had to wave a bulletin in her face to revive her. The Reverent rampaged off to instruct another poor sinner in the error of his ways.

"You will burn in the fire that never dies!" he screamed at Mr. Huber. Rumor has it the Reverend once caught Mr. Huber in the public library reading *The Bhagavad Gita*, the Hindu scriptures. Shoot, if you're going to do that, you might as well get a shovel and start digging a hole down to Hell right now, because that's the only faster way to get there.

The Reverend ran down the aisle. He didn't stop until the microphone cord nearly jerked him off his feet. He eyed us in the back as if he knew the only reason we were sitting there was to avoid him, which was true. He ran back up the aisle again.

What I didn't understand was, except for maybe Mrs. O'Reilly and Mr. Huber, who the Reverend was always screaming at. There weren't any Muslims, Buddhists, Hindus, Catholics, or Jews in the congregation, and after listening to him, I didn't blame them. Nobody likes to be told to go to Hell. Not by someone who means it, anyway.

The Reverend climbed up behind the pulpit, put the microphone back in its stand, and started beating it silly again. I quit paying attention. That kind of thing was funny once in a while, but it got tiresome week after week.

My bulletin was filled in. I was out of things to do. If I'd been with Clint and Jeff, we'd be ogling Mrs. Kramer's sweaty religious ecstasy, but no, this Sunday I had to sit in the back. I was getting pretty bored.

So I pinched Jackey.

"Ouch!"

"Shh. We're in church."

"But you pinched me!"

"No I didn't."

53

"Yes you did!" He pinched me back, the little twerp. I couldn't just let him get away with that, so I gave him a kick. Jackey's legs were too short to reach mine, so he elbow jabbed me in the ribs. As I cocked my arm back to punch him, I felt Dad's hand close over my fist. Like I said, next to Ello Tohrey, Dad had the biggest hands in the world.

"If you two don't settle down," he whispered, "next week you'll spend the whole service standing in the foyer."

"Big deal." The ushers stood in the foyer every service. Sometimes they played cards.

"The big deal is your butts will be so sore from the lashing I'll give them this week, you still won't be to sit down *next* week."

No argument from me. Neither of us moved for the rest of the service.

When it was finally over, the congregation emptied into the foyer. Everyone stood around in patches, and a half dozen smiling people wove back and forth between them like needles patching a quilt. Me and Dad and Jackey waited by the choir's practice room.

"How'd it sound?" Mom asked when she came out.

"What, the sermon?" Dad was teasing her.

"No, the anthem."

"Oh. Really fine."

"It needed more bass, didn't it?"

"Well . . ."

"I'm telling you, John, we could really use your voice in the choir." Dad didn't say anything. He never did when she suggested that.

Mom led us to the door. Dad brought up the rear. Mom always led us everywhere.

Someone tugged my sleeve. It was Jeff. His face was flushed and his eyes glazed. He looked the same way Moses must have looked when he came down the mountain after seeing the burning bush.

"The blue one," he panted. "And you should have seen her sweat. She was just *dripping*."

"Oh, man!"

"And there's more. She demonstrated to the fat alto that sits next to her the cut on a new pink dress she just bought. It goes even lower than the blue one."

"Oh, man!"

"Sweaty pink is more see-through than sweaty blue."

"Oh, man!" I knew I was repeating myself, but just the thought of it froze my brain up. Dad had to guide me to the exit.

The Reverend Carstairs stood at the door, smiling as much as he was capable of. He shook everyone's hand, even the smallest kid. His handshake wasn't anything like Ello Tohrey's. It was more like shaking a fish—a warm, wet, dead fish.

"Praise the Lord!" he said to Jackey. Jackey didn't answer.

"And you, too!" I didn't answer, either.

"Nice sermon," Dad said as he walked by.

"I'm praying for the souls of you and your family," the Reverend said.

"Don't pray for our souls, Reverend." Dad looked at the sky. "Pray for rain."

"Don't fret over worldly things, Jack," the Reverend said. "It is written in the Good Book that 'Man does not live by bread alone, but by every word that issues forth from the mouth of God.'"

"That's easy for Him to say. He doesn't have to eat."

Mom reached back and took Dad's arm. "God will provide," she said as she yanked him down the steps. That's what she always said when things looked tough.

God will provide.

After church, we went to Grampa and Gramma's for dinner. We always did. They went to the Methodist church and were always done before us, especially in the winter. Their minister liked to get home in time for the football game.

"Hi, Jack. Abby." Grampa stood from his chair as we came through the door.

"No," Mom said, "sit."

Grampa grunted. "I'm not so old I can't get up when family comes through the door." He walked halfway across the room, the whole time leaning heavily on his cane. He slapped Jackey on the back as Jackey bolted by him, then shook my hand. His hands were big like Dad's, but not callused. All the calluses were wrinkled off.

"I see you have your garden in," Dad said. "Looks good."

"Looks good now." Grampa grunted again as he sat back down. "It might not look so good later. Have to see what the weather does."

Grampa's name was August Thomas Morrell. During World War II, he saved his platoon by shoving a grenade through the gun slot of a German pillbox. Afterward, the Germans overran his position, and he had to play dead until it was dark enough to crawl back through their lines. He was shot four times and his legs froze; that's why he walked with a cane. He won the Medal of Valor.

Grampa never called World War II anything but "The War." Everybody knew which war he meant. For Grampa, there were no other wars, not real ones anyway. Not even Vietnam, the war Uncle Eugene died in.

I sat on the couch, beneath a photograph of the farm back during the black-and-white days. Grampa and Gramma's house was full of stuff like that: old pictures, old pottery, even a horse harness on the porch. The house smelled of old stuff, too—old leather and stale bread and the funny smells of the liniments Grampa put on his legs—old-people smells.

Mom followed Jackey past Grampa into the kitchen. Jackey went straight for Gramma's cookie jar. As he snitched one, Gramma slapped his hand.

"I don't know what's with children nowadays," she complained. "They're either little beggars or little thieves."

"Maybe you should eliminate the temptation." Mom put the jar on top of the refrigerator. Gramma waited until Mom turned her back, then put it down where Jackey could reach it. When he took another one, she patted his head.

Old people. If they're not already dead, they're half crazy.

Gramma made up the gravy, and when it was ready we all sat down to dinner—roast beef, potatoes, and corn, with blueberry pie for dessert. After dinner, Mom and Gramma went into the kitchen to do dishes. Me and Jackey and Dad and Grampa hefted our bloated bellies into the living room. Grampa sat in his chair and lit up his pipe. Dad went for Gramma's rocker, and me and Jackey the couch. Jackey fell asleep as soon as his butt hit the cushion.

We sat that way for a long time, not really saying anything. Grampa muttered and chuckled as he puffed on his pipe. Dad sat in the chair with his back straight and his hands clasped in his lap. He looked like someone who'd been sent to the principal's office. He always looked that way around Grampa—I don't know why. I think it had something to do with the farm.

Gramma came in. Dad got out of her chair and sat next to me on the couch.

"Clare," Grampa asked, "do you remember that Fourth of July when the bird crapped in your brother Ernie's mouth?"

"Of course, August." Gramma picked up her knitting. She was making a pair of baby shoes for one of a neighbor's kids.

"Wasn't that the funniest thing you ever saw?"

"Of course, August." Gramma kept knitting. She could talk to Grampa without hearing a word he said.

Grampa laughed and puffed on his pipe, smiling. He looked at Dad. "How are my fields?"

Dad shrugged. "Like your garden. They're all right now, but this weather might be hard on them."

Grampa grunted. "I remember helping your grand-dad during the drought of thirty-six. It was so dry, dust suffocated half our livestock. It gathered around the house like snowdrifts. And the grasshoppers—good Lord, there haven't been such grasshoppers since

Moses. You think you have it bad."

Dad didn't say anything. His leg pressed against mine. The muscles in it were pulled as taut as bowstrings. His hands were clenched so tightly, his knuckles were white.

Grampa leaned back in his chair and gazed at the ceiling. He drifted into his "philosophical mode," as Mom called it. "The way I see things," he said, "if you work a piece of land long enough, it takes on your personality. It even starts to look like you. I worked that land for thirty years. Now it's like me—tough, durable, productive." A puff of blue smoke rose from his lips. "Handsome."

"That's the biggest crock of bull I've ever heard," Gramma said.

"What, dear?"

"Nothing, August." Grampa was hard of hearing, and Gramma took advantage of it. You had to be careful around him with cracks like that.

Mom came in, wiping her hands on a towel, and sat across from us. Everyone except me started heeing and hawing about the farm. Pretty soon I got sleepy. Everything just sort of faded away, and when it all faded back in again I was sitting in the backseat of the car. We were almost home.

I rubbed my eyes and leaned over the front seat. "What did you guys do after I fell asleep?" I asked.

"Nothing much," Mom said. "Just talked."

"Talked about what?"

"The farm." Dad's shoulders tensed. His fingers gripped the wheel as if he was trying to squeeze blood out of it. "He doesn't understand," he muttered.

Mom laid her hand on his arm. "Now honey, he is your father."

"I know." Dad didn't say anything else until he turned into the driveway. "But he still doesn't understand."

CHAPTER FIVE

Farmers cultivate to break up the soil and kill the weeds. The real bummer part of cultivation is that it kills only the weeds growing between the rows, not the ones in them. It's not that big a deal with corn because corn grows tall, but soybeans grow close to the ground, and if you leave the weeds in, they'll choke the beans out.

What that means is that every summer someone has to walk the beans and pull the weeds. On the Morrell farm "someone" always meant me. I hated walking beans. I really did.

If you ever want to find a beanwalker, drive out on a country road and search the fields for someone with a hoe who looks like his parents died and his wife left him and a truck hit his dog and his baby was born looking like Mr. Potato Head. Search for total misery. When you find it, you've found a beanwalker.

Me and Dad and Mom walked our four hundred acres, then rented ourselves out to the neighbors to earn a little extra money. We spent a lot of time on George Shade's property. George bought out the Millers and the Hedstroms when the bank foreclosed on them. Now his fields stretched to Heaven and back.

One day toward the end of July, we were walking Little Crow's field. Little Crow's was a long, narrow hundred and eighty acres, running east to west. It was late afternoon, and the only things overhead were the blue and the sun. The only things that had been overhead all summer were the blue and the sun. It was so hot my ears whistled, so hot the corn in the distance frolicked in the heat like demons dancing in a nightmare. We were walking through Hell. No lie.

I was out a little in front of Mom and Dad, heading west into the sun. My wrists draped over the hoe handle as it lay across my shoulders. Milkweed sap gummed up my gloves—there's no stickier goo in all the world than that. The dust rose in clouds every time I took a step. It settled in the scratches on my arms and clotted in the back of my throat. I was dirty and sticky and sweaty and thirsty all at the same time. I felt so miserable I wanted to die.

Three crows flew by. They looked down and cawed, laughing at me. I threw a stone, but there's no way I can hit a crow in flight, so I pretended to shoot them with my hoe. They just laughed some more and went off to play in the trees.

And Charlie Darwin said we're the intelligent species.

In the middle of the field was the hill where Chief Little Crow stood during the Sioux uprising. It was the highest point in the county; from the top you could see everywhere. You could see the fields for miles and the sledding hill and the Tohreys' roof above the trees. You could see all the way to where George Shade's fields ended, and sometimes at night you could see the glow from Elder Falls. That hill was the top of the world.

"There are parts of the universe," Clint always said, "that even people will never be able to screw up." Little Crow's hill was one of them.

Every year the wind carried summer smells up the hill. Sometimes the wind was so full of the green in the fields and pastures, it made my head spin. This summer when I reached the top, it wasn't that way. Nothing was green this summer.

The sun had burned everything.

I mean *everything*. The beans were yellow and the corn was yellow and the grass was dying in the pastures. Nothing was growing, nothing was alive enough to *be* growing. The smell on the wind was a dry smell, like the smell of leaves crackling in a fire.

There was no life in it; there was no life anywhere. The only things living were the souls of me and Mom and Dad, and when your soul knows everything around it is dying, it thinks it's dying, too. It gets so lonely it wants to cry, and even if you want to feel happy you can't. You want to cry, too.

That's how I felt, standing there. I didn't have an ounce of water in my whole body, but tears built up in my eyes. One rolled down to my lip. It tasted salty.

"You missed one." Mom stood four rows over from me, leaning on her hoe. She had a heavy gray streak across her forehead. I reached down and pulled up an elephant ear.

"What's wrong?" she asked as I stood. I didn't know what to say. What was wrong was too big for words. I just knew I wanted to get away from there. I just knew I didn't want to feel lonely anymore.

"Well?" she asked.

"How come I have to be out here?"

"What do you mean?"

"I don't like this, Mom. Everything's dying."

"We have work to do. When the work is done, you can leave."

"But I don't want to be out here."

"Quit your whining."

Whining? She thought I was whining? I was screaming, I was crying, but I wasn't whining. The emptiness built up in me like a tidal wave. It crashed

65

against my soul, and the only way for it to get out was through my words, and I didn't have the words to release it.

"Damn it, Mom—"

"Watch your mouth!"

"But Mom, if you'll just listen—"

"I don't ever want to hear you say that again! God's children don't talk that way!" The cords in her neck stood out like guitar strings. Her eyes went wild. I'd only seen her look like that once before. It was right after Aunt Maggie died.

Dad came up the hill. He wiped the sweat off his forehead and rested his chin on the butt end of his hoe. He looked at the sky and shook his head, then stared across the field and shook his head again.

"Did you hear what your son just said?" Mom asked.

Dad didn't answer.

"Did you?"

He still didn't answer. He stared across the field, then trudged down the hill toward the road.

"Dad, you missed a ragweed."

"Forget the ragweed."

"But John," Mom said, "there's still another hour before supper. We could almost finish the field—"

"Forget the field."

"John?"

He reached down to pull off a yellow soybean

leaf. He rolled it between his fingers, then let it fall dead to the ground. He didn't look up. "We're done. There's nothing worth saving, anyway."

He cut across the rows to the road, then crossed it and walked up the driveway. Every time he took a step, gray dust rose from his boots. Me and Mom watched him until he was halfway to the house; then we followed.

CHAPTER SIX

By the time school rolled around and I had to put my life on hold for another nine months, all the chicks we'd bought were little hens and roosters. Jackey was so proud, I thought he'd bust. He didn't know that most of them would be butchered before winter, and I wasn't about to tell him. He probably wouldn't want to feed them anymore, and if he didn't, I'd have to. I had enough to do as it was.

After school during the harvest I had to help Dad in the fields. While we worked, he didn't joke or laugh or even sing. He just sat on the tractor, glancing over his shoulder every now and then at the beans as they were picked. I have to admit there wasn't much to be cheery about. It was the most pitiful crop you ever saw. We barely made enough money to cover the cost of harvesting it.

The day we finished, I went up to my room. I had so much homework to do, it made me sick. I had to write a paper for English about my favorite author and I didn't have any favorite authors. I had to read about the Revolutionary War for history and do twenty problems for math. What a waste of time.

What's so great about authors? They're a bunch of sissies too stupid to do anything but sit around picking their noses until they're bored enough to write a book. Take this Mark Twain guy. He got so bored, he floated down the Mississippi River on a raft, and then he was stupid enough to think someone might want to *read* about it. And where'd he get a goofball name like Huckleberry Finn? If that's the best he could come up with, he should've just kept floating until he was lost at sea. How many parents look at their newborn baby boy in the hospital and say, "Let's name him Huckleberry?" What's the matter with Bob or Tim?

Mark Twain's real name was Samuel Clemens. He was so embarrassed about what he did for a living, he changed his *name*.

And history is about as useful. What my teacher expected me to learn from the Revolutionary War is way beyond me. Back then they didn't have TV, they didn't have radios, they didn't have anything. What could they know? So we had a war and a bunch of people died. Big deal. I didn't know any of them.

School can be so stupid sometimes that if I didn't have to do the homework, it would make me laugh. Sometimes I laugh anyway.

Four backfires like old dinosaur farts told me Ello Tohrey was coming to visit. That guy didn't own anything made this century. I heard his truck stop and he laughed as he crossed the yard. He and Dad talked on the porch.

Jackey came in and flopped down on his bed. "I was out looking at the chickens," he said.

"Big deal."

"Chester don't look so good."

"What do you expect? He never gets enough to eat." He. She. I wished Jackey had picked a better name for that silly bird.

"It's all Cleo's fault. Darn old Cleo eats like a pig and Chester's starving to death. What sense does that make?"

I didn't answer. I couldn't explain chicken logic to him, even if I wanted to. There's probably not a man alive who can.

Jackey started reading a comic book, but it was one he'd read a ba-zillion times, so he put it down again. "I'm going to build a pen for Chester."

"No you're not. Don't you remember the pecking order thing?"

"I'm in charge of the chickens. What I say goes." He pulled an old toy tractor out from under the bed, then lay on his back and ran it back and forth across his chest. "Where's Mom?" he asked.

"At church."

"She's always at church."

"I know." And when she wasn't, she was talking to the Reverend on the phone. She was getting a little cuckoo on the religion thing.

Another truck rumbled up the driveway. Jackey jumped to the window.

"Who is it?"

"Mr. Shade. I'll see what's up." He bounded out the door. By the time I got to the kitchen, he was heading back upstairs again.

"What's going on?"

"Dad said to go find something to do."

"Why?"

"I don't know." He blew a booger in his hand and wiped it off behind his knee. Like I said, he was gross. "Do you want to play a game of Parcheesi?"

"Set it up. I'll be there in a minute." Jackey ran upstairs and I went into the living room. Through the open porch door I saw George sitting on the railing, leaning against the screen. I sat down and listened.

"Hard year for you, huh Jack?" George asked.

"Hard year for everybody," Dad said.

"I'm glad you're here, Ello," George went on. "My proposition concerns you, too." Ello grunted. He

71

didn't like George. When they came together neither one would give in—the irresistible object meeting the immovable force.

"I want to buy the woods along the property line between the two of you," George said.

"Why?" Dad asked.

"With development, it could become a pretty little park, or maybe a wildlife refuge. It would put a few dollars in your pockets and fulfill my desire to preserve the environment."

"Bull," Ello said.

"What?"

"I said bull. You bought the woodlot on the Hansen place. Now a lumber outfit's clearing it. That doesn't sound too environmental to me."

"I'm having them take down a few diseased trees—"

"You're having them clearcut it. George, how dumb do you think we are? You'll clearcut our land, sell the timber, and make a profit—"

"That would be stupid," George interrupted. "The land would cost more than the timber could ever possibly be worth."

"Let me finish. After you sell the timber, you'll get an investment credit. Then you'll tell the government that the ground you cleared was for cash crops, but you'll be conscientious and set it aside to lie fallow. They'll pay you for taking it out of production. You end up with the value of the timber, an investment credit, and governmental reimbursement for fallow land. You rape the land and get paid three times for it."

George was silent for a moment. "That never occurred to me."

"Then why are you clearcutting the Hansens'?"

Nobody said anything for a long time. Ello seemed too mad to and George too embarrassed. Dad never talked all that much anyway.

"My part of the woods isn't for sale," Dad finally said.

Ello grunted again. "Mine either."

George stood. "You can't blame me for trying, can you?"

"I imagine I can blame you for a lot of things," Ello said.

"Maybe I should leave."

"There's an idea."

"No," Dad said, "we're neighbors; let's act like neighbors. But please don't come to me with a suggestion like that again." He paused. "You want a beer?"

"No, I can't stay long. Actually though, now that I'm here, when's the last time I mentioned I want to buy your farm?"

"The last time you visited."

"Have you considered my offer?"

"Yes."

"And?"

"And I can't sell you my farm."

George sighed. "You can't fool me, Jack. After a year like this, if you don't sell to me, the bank will take it, and if the bank takes it, I'll just buy it from them."

"Shut up, Shade," Ello said. "There's no need for talk like that."

"How much are you in debt, Jack?" George asked, ignoring Ello.

"None of your business," Ello growled.

"I can speak for myself." Dad cleared his throat. "Enough."

"Are they going to foreclose on you?"

"Not this year."

"But they're going to."

Dad didn't say anything.

"If you sell to me," George said, "you'll save yourself the embarrassment of foreclosure and me the inconvenience of buying your farm from the bank. We'll both come out ahead."

"Maybe," Dad said, "but I won't sell."

"Why not?"

"Because when I was five, my grandfather took me down to the creek and showed me where the foundations of the first Morrell cabin were laid. When my sons were five, their grandfather showed them the same thing. A Morrell cleared this land. Morrells have died on it. If I gave it up, I'd be cutting every tie I have with who I am. And it would kill my dad."

Mine, too, I thought.

"I hate to sound hard," George said, "but one way or another, I'll end up with it. I've always considered you a friend, Jack. I'm just trying to save us both some heartache."

"Selling this farm would be more heartache than I could stand."

George sighed. "All right, that's all I wanted to know. I'll be leaving." He stepped down the stairs.

"Are you sure you don't want a beer?" Dad asked.

"No, thanks. By the way, I drove by your fields as I came over. Nothing's growing out there anymore."

"Nothing's been growing out there all summer," Dad said quietly, too quietly for George to hear.

The gravel pinged against the pickup's fenders as George drove away. I stood to go upstairs. Jackey would have Parcheesi set up by now, and if I didn't get up there pretty soon, he'd holler. I took a step, but something Dad said made me stop dead.

"I'm going to lose the farm, Ello."

"Don't talk that way."

"Even if Abby goes to full-time at the nursing home, we won't be able to make the payments this fall. And she won't go full-time. Remember how she was after her sister died? She's getting . . . funny . . . again."

"Have you talked to the Farmers Home Administration?"

Dad sighed. "What good would that do? They won't give me another loan. Besides, I've had it with government handouts."

"They keep us alive."

"Hardly. This year they're subsidizing sixty-five percent of my lost crop. How am I supposed to survive on that?"

"You could get another job. I hear Mercer's is hiring." Mercer's was a printing company on the outskirts of Elder Falls.

"Have you ever worked there?" Dad asked.

"For a year once, when Lois was sick. I worked nights and farmed during the day. It was tough."

"At least my harvest is in."

"It'll still be tough."

"I heard people get hurt."

"I saw a guy's hand get sucked between the printing rollers. They squashed his arm to paste all the way up to his elbow. Snapped off three of his fingers. You have to be careful."

"I'm not a printer," Dad said. "I'm a farmer."

"You're not alone. I have to get a second job, too."

"At Mercer's?"

"My brother-in-law is getting me in at the canning company in Owatonna."

"Are any other jobs open there?"

"There are a lot of farmers looking for extra work. It'll take everything he has just to get *me* in." They were quiet again.

Jackey banged across the floor above me. I hurried on tippy-toes into the kitchen. He was standing at the head of the stairs. I raised my finger to my lips.

"What are we being quiet for?" he whispered.

"We're just being quiet."

I didn't want Dad to know I'd been eavesdropping. I don't think he'd have punished me, but it didn't make any difference. I didn't want him to know.

CHAPTER SEVEN

Dad got a night job, from eleven to seven, at Mercer's. When I asked him what he did, he said he was a jogger. I didn't know what he meant, so he explained it to me.

Printing presses can be as big as three-story buildings. The paper starts off on one end in rolls almost as tall as a man. It's fed through a series of presses, one press for each color. In the presses, the ink is transferred to a plate, then a roller, and finally to the paper. The paper is dried in an oven, then cut and folded, coming out of the press on the other end. From there it's stacked on pallets and sent to the bindery, where it's glued together into magazines or catalogs.

Joggers stack the paper on the pallets in bundles neat enough for the bindery to use. They do this by bouncing a handful of paper on end and compressing it like an accordion to get air between the pages. The air allows the papers to slip over each other. When the joggers are done, instead of the papers going every which way, the bundles are neat little blocks with straight sides, almost like bricks.

Jogging must be the worst job at the plant. It sure doesn't sound very glamorous.

Dad came home every morning while we were eating breakfast. He'd have ink in his hair and on his face and soaked through his clothes from cleaning the presses. His forearms would be red from a bazillion paper cuts, and sometimes they'd be bleeding. As soon as he was done with breakfast, he'd head out the door again and do the farmwork. If he was lucky, he'd be stumbling to bed about the time me and Jackey got home from school. If he wasn't lucky, he wouldn't be. Sometimes he didn't sleep at all.

One Saturday morning he came home and went straight to bed. He didn't even stop for breakfast.

"I thought he was going to plow and butcher chickens today," I said.

"He's going to sleep." Mom filled the big boiler with water. "He's worked enough."

"After all me and Jackey did, we better butcher today." We'd blocked off the coop's chicken door and for the last two nights had been using chicken hooks to snare the roosters and hens out of their roosts in the trees. We had to do it at night when they were sleeping. They were too quick to catch during the day.

"We can butcher the chickens ourselves," Mom said.

"Just me and you?"

"And Jackey."

"You're going to let Jackey handle a knife?"

"He can fetch the chickens for us."

I put my cereal bowl in the sink. "Does Dad have tonight off?"

"Yes."

"Can we go into town and see a movie?"

"No."

"Why not?"

"Because money's tight and movies are expensive. Besides, they aren't good for you."

I stared at her. "Huh?"

"Movies are filled with the sins of the flesh. I won't have my boys being led astray—not by movies, not by anything. Now go out and do the chores. I'll start the water boiling."

When I walked by the coop, I saw that Jackey had Chester's feeding pen done. It was nothing more than a chicken-wire box with a little gate held shut by a paper clip—exactly the kind of handiwork you'd expect from an eight-year-old.

Only two chickens were in sight: Cleo scratched

in the dirt and Chester peeked out from under the storage shed. Jackey stood with the top of his head against the coop door, staring at the ground.

"Are we going to kill them all?" His voice was tiny.

"We'll leave half the year-old hens for layers. When we're done, there should be twenty blue-banded hens left." We banded the legs of our chickens. The red we'd banded two years ago; the blue, one.

"Which ones are going to live?"

"That's for you to decide. Your job will be to fetch them to the chopping block."

When he looked at me, his eyes were teary. "I don't wanna do it. I really don't wanna do it."

"You have to. We have to eat."

"We can eat eggs."

"Not all the time." I went to the storage shed and came back with a hatchet. Its blade flashed in the sun.

"I won't pick Chester," Jackey said. He was staring at the ground.

"Chester's not in the coop. You couldn't catch her now, even if you wanted to."

"Yes I could. Chester gets so scared, she freezes up. Gramma could catch her."

"Well, I wouldn't kill her if you did. She'd be too stringy to eat."

The kitchen door slammed. Mom came out with

81

the boiler. The steam rising from it dampened her hair. She dumped it in a sawed-off fifty-five-gallon drum by the garage.

"You might as well get started," she called.

"All right." I opened the coop door, but Jackey slammed it shut again.

"Can we give them a last meal?"

"Why? It's a waste of feed."

"They give murderers last meals. Not a single chicken in that coop has ever murdered anyone, and you want to send them to Heaven hungry. You have a black heart."

I sighed. "I'll get the feed pail." I went to the shed and came back with some corn. Jackey trudged into the coop like a mourner at Santa Claus' funeral. I took the hatchet to the chopping block and buried its blade in its surface. I liked the *thunk!* sound it made.

"Bring one out here, Jackey!"

Squawking came from the coop, and white wings brushed against its window. A minute later Jackey came out, holding a fat hen by her ankles. She screamed like the heroine in a cheap horror movie. Chickens aren't dumb. She knew what was coming.

"Will this one do?" Jackey tried to hold her away from his body, but her flapping wings beat him silly anyway.

"She'll do." I took her neck and held her head on the block. White wings flashed against the coop window. The chickens inside were trying to watch. They reminded me of the French nobility staring out of their prison windows as Marie Marionette went to her execution. We were studying the French Revolution in history.

"Stand back, Jackey." He did.

I raised the hatchet straight up in the air, like a guillotine blade. I felt pretty good. I'd found a use for history.

"Eat *this* cake, Marie." The hatchet flashed again, and then I brought it down.

Thunk!

I jumped back as fast as I could. So did Jackey. After you cut a chicken's head off, it doesn't just lie down and die like you'd think it would. It hops around, spraying blood everywhere, as if the thought suddenly occurs to it that it better get in as much living as it can before it can't move anymore.

I wonder if Marie flopped when she died. I bet *that* was something to see.

When I beheaded the second one, a rooster, he did the same thing. A couple more thunks and we had a bloody chorus line in the yard. It wasn't long before I had thirty chicken heads piled next to the stump and red splotches all over me. When we were down to twenty blue banded, I signaled Jackey. He opened the chicken door in the coop, and the surviving hens streamed out like prisoners from the

Bastille. If chickens can weep joyful tears, they were doing it.

Mom and I gathered up the bodies that had quit flopping. We soaked them in the drum for a few minutes, loosening their feathers. Plucking isn't bad, except boiled feathers don't smell very good and there's nothing grosser than picking a chicken's butt.

Pretty soon a long row of headless, naked chickens lay on the picnic table. Mom went to get the knives. The cats gathered around, mewing. One jumped up next to the chickens. I waved it off.

"Keep these cats away from here, Jackey. That's your new job." He ran around the table, shooing and kicking. He didn't look at the dead chickens.

Mom came back with two knives and a boiler full of clean water. We went to work, getting the chickens ready for the freezer. When we slit them open, their guts spilled out like warm, steamy spaghetti.

I've always liked chicken guts. It amazes me that a pile of goo like that can do everything it does. It digests food and turns it into energy and meat. It breathes and it pumps blood and it leaves little white droppings all over the yard. It makes *baby chickens*, if you can believe it. That just blows my mind.

"Don't forget to save the gizzards," Mom said. "You know how your grandpa likes gizzards."

"I won't." But I would have if she hadn't mentioned it.

Since chickens don't have teeth, they swallow gravel into their gizzards to grind their food. I used to have these metal army men I'd play in the driveway with. Once I cut a gizzard open and found two of them in there, as if they were waiting in ambush. Pretty amazing.

I was just starting on my third chicken when who should come wandering out of the pasture but old Muddle-Head. He had on this ragged pair of coveralls with only one shoulder strap. The crotch hung almost to his knees. You'll never see Muddle-Head on the cover of GQ.

"Hello, Merle." Mom smiled at him. She would. She was always going around encouraging people like him to stay ignorants. Not me. I made sure they knew where I stood right off the bat.

"Hey, old Muddle-Head," I said. "What's the matter, the funny farm closed for the weekend?"

Mom's eyes just about popped out of her head, rolled across the table, and slapped me across the cheek. Because they couldn't, her hand did. Hard. I just stared at her. "What was that for?"

"You know what that was for. I never want to hear you talk like that to Merle again. Now apologize."

Merle stood by the end of the table, watching us. "I'm sorry," I said, but I wasn't. I mean, when you're right, you're right, and when you're right you have to say what's on your mind, even if it means getting slapped. That's what I think, anyway.

I turned back to the chicken. I plunged the knife in, ran it up to the chest, and watched the guts tumble out. All of a sudden Muddle-Head started whimpering. I looked up at him. He was watching me.

"It's just a chicken, Mu—" I stopped. Mom threw her gaze at me like she was wielding a flamethrower. "It's just a chicken, Merle," I said.

But that didn't make any difference to Muddle-Head. He started crying, and then Jackey started crying, too. Mom put her arm around his shoulder. Muddle-Head reached into the bib of his overalls and took out this little teddy bear. He clutched it to his chest and drooled on it.

"Hey," I shouted, "that's mine!"

Mom looked at the teddy. "You're right. I wonder how he got that."

"He probably came in the house when we weren't home and took it. You know how he is." I stood up. "Give it back, Muddle-Head!"

Mom whacked me again. Jesus Criminey, what was she slapping *me* for? I wasn't the thief.

"But Mom, he stole it!"

"That's no reason to call him names."

"But that's mine!"

"You haven't used it for years. You probably didn't even know you still owned it."

What difference did that make? "But Mom . . ."

"If Merle can use it, what harm is there in letting him?"

I sat back down and went to work. Some people just didn't understand anything. Who cared if I didn't know I still owned it? Who cared if he could use it? And who even cared if I'd never use it again? It was still mine. But just try telling that to Mom. She was into this Christian charity thing, like that's the way the world operates. I told you she was going cuckoo.

I hacked at the chicken as much as I could, getting blood everywhere, making a mess of it, just because I knew Muddle-Head wouldn't like it if I did. After he finally wandered back into the pasture, still whimpering, I hacked up the thighs like Jack the Ripper. Mom liked dark meat.

We worked for a couple hours. I didn't say anything. What could I say? Every time I opened my mouth, I was getting slapped. So I just worked. Jackey quit crying. Mom hummed church hymns.

"I want you boys to stay out of the house," Mom said when we were just about through. "Let your father sleep." She tossed a liver into the boiler. Her hands were red and slimy. I'd been watching her clean chickens since I was a little kid, but I still couldn't picture her doing it. Butchering isn't something Southern Baptist Southern Belles do.

"Well?" she asked.

"All right."

"You hear me, Jackey?"

"Yeah, Mom." When the cats weren't keeping him busy, he stood at the end of the table, his head down. It was pretty tough on him, the poor little guy. It's hard to watch something you've cared for die like that.

"Come here, Jackey." I picked up another chicken. "I want to show you something."

I held the chicken so it stood on the table. "Now watch what happens when you squeeze their legs together real fast." I pulled them apart and slammed them back together, like a bellows. The chicken crowed. Even without a head, it crowed. Dead chickens are so cool.

"Mama," Jackey cried, "make him stop!"

I stared at him. "What—"

"Quit teasing your brother," Mom said.

"I was just trying to—"

"I don't care what you were trying to do. Quit teasing your brother."

I put the chicken down. Jackey ran around the corner of the house, crying.

Well excuse me for living. I was just trying to cheer the little twerp up. It seemed I couldn't do anything right that day. Jeez.

We were just finishing up the last two when Dad came out the kitchen door. He had his coveralls on.

"Why aren't you sleeping?" Mom asked.

"I can't sleep when there's plowing to do." He

rubbed his eyes. "How are the chickens coming?"

"Almost done."

"Good." He walked past the table toward the utility shed where we kept the tractor. I watched him go.

Mom had said no, but maybe Dad wouldn't. It was worth a shot.

"Dad, can we go to the movies tonight?"

"Thomas!" Mom glared at me. It was the same kind of glare Marietta gave Clint when he called the Reverend Carstairs "mister."

Dad stopped. "I don't see why not. You're working hard today. We all could use a break."

"John!" Now she glared at Dad. "I won't have my children going to those movies! They're the devil's work!"

"What?" Dad looked baffled. "You never used to—"

"I don't care if I never used to. Those films are evil."

"But Dad, you already said—"

"We'll play miniature golf instead." His eyes never left Mom's face. "Is there anything in your Bible that says we can't knock a little ball into a clown's mouth?"

Mom's lips got real tight and thin. She stood up and stomped into the house. Dad went to plow, and I finished the chickens.

We played three rounds of miniature golf that night. I won twice and Jackey once. Dad came in last every time. He wasn't much when it came to miniature golf.

Mom didn't go. She said she wanted to pray.

CHAPTER EIGHT

Dad finished plowing before the snow came. We only had a dusting for Thanksgiving, not even enough to whiten the furrows in the fields. It was cold though, but not the kind of cold that waits like a dog to bite your nose as soon as you step out the door. That kind of cold always came later, in January and February.

Mom drove in to the grocery store the Monday before Thanksgiving. She came back with bags and bags of potatoes and stuffing and sweet potatoes and pie filling. She bought a twenty-pound turkey. It was so huge I broke into a sweat carrying it in from the car.

"I want a special Thanksgiving," Mom said. "I want to express to The Good Lord Above how thankful we are for all our Bountiful Blessings." That's how she said it. With capitals.

91

I didn't mind. I'd thank the devil if he showed up at the door with a twenty-pound turkey. I like turkey.

Mom invited Grampa and Gramma Morrell out for Thanksgiving dinner. She also invited the Reverend Carstairs.

"Why?" I asked. I figured the Reverend would want to spend Thanksgiving however he usually did. I bet he went over to Marietta's house and bounced Bible verses off her forehead.

"Because he's the shepherd of the flock and we should show our appreciation."

That whole shepherd-and-flock thing doesn't wash with me. I'm no sheep. Sheep don't have the good sense God gave a dung beetle. You'd think that when it's raining and the barn door's wide open, sheep would go inside, but no, you have to go out and lead them in. If you don't, they'll stand out there in all their idiotic glory until they drown. They're that dumb.

And religious people call me a sheep. I consider it an insult.

About ten o'clock Thursday morning, Grampa and Gramma's car pulled into the driveway. Three seconds later Gramma was bustling around the kitchen with her apron on, clucking like a fat hen over her brood. While Dad and Grampa walked around the farm, she and Mom busied themselves cooking.

Mom busied herself cooking, anyway; Gramma just busied herself. The only cooking she bothered with was cooking Mom had already done. Take the stuffing, for example. Mom got it just the way she wanted it; then while she was working on the sweet potatoes, Gramma added more sage and onion without telling her. That's the way Gramma did things. She was sneaky.

The meal was ready at noon, but the Reverend hadn't shown up. Everybody sat in the living room staring at each other, all thinking the same thing. The rich smells of melted butter and onion and pumpkin pie lolled around our heads. The turkey warmed in the oven, drying out.

"I'm hungry," Jackey whined.

"So am I." My stomach growled. "Does he know what time dinner is?"

"Yes," Mom said.

"Then where is he?"

"I guess he's late." It didn't take Sherlock Holmes to figure that out. "His eyes are poor. Maybe he's having trouble driving out here."

I knew that was baloney. Reverend Carstairs might have looked like he was going blind, but I knew for a fact he could see when he wanted to. Once, during the sermon, Clint penciled a "666" on his forehead. I could barely see it sitting right next to him, but when the Reverend glanced our way, his mouth dropped open like he'd seen a Hindu motorcycle gang beating up Mary Magdalene. So don't tell me his eyes were poor. If he had trouble driving, it was because being late made him feel important.

You have to watch old guys. If you give them the chance, they'll pull stuff like that on you every time.

At half past twelve, the Reverend's big fancy Lincoln pulled up, and Mom went to answer the door. That car was the most beautiful thing you could ever hope to see. It had thick maroon upholstery and a really nice stereo and power everything. If the angels drive cars in Heaven, they drive ones like the Reverend's. They drive Lincolns and play harps. In Hell, the demons have scooters and kazoos.

Clint asked the Reverend once why Jesus allowed him to drive a Lincoln when he told the rich young ruler to give everything he had away. The Reverend said he would like to give everything away, but he wasn't young like the ruler was. He had to prepare himself for Heaven's riches.

That might just be true. I'm sure if you're not ready for it, the shock of seeing the pearly gates would kill you on the spot.

"PRAISE THE LORD!"

"Praise the Lord, Reverend," Mom said. "I'm glad you could make it." She led him into the living room.

"PRAISE THE LORD!" the Reverend bellowed again. None of us answered him. Grampa and Dad

94

looked like they were losing their appetites. I was feeling a bit queasy myself.

"I pray God's grace down upon this house," the Reverend said, "and on all his children gathered herein. May the Lord bless us while we partake of his bounty. May he protect us from the Evil One."

In my opinion, the Evil One had just walked through the door. Anybody responsible for drying out a good turkey can't be a saint.

We went to the dining room. I sat in my usual place in the corner. Grampa hooked his cane over my chair and tried to sit at the head of the table, where he always sat, but the Reverend shouldered his way in first. Before Grampa could say anything, Gramma signaled him to take a different chair. Grampa looked at the ceiling, sighed, and sat down next to me.

"Pass the potatoes," he said.

The Reverend stood up again and closed his eyes. "Oh Lord," he prayed, "I seek your blessing on these your children . . ."

"Good God," Dad groaned. The Reverend took that as fervent approval. The same thing happened with the moaning in church. He fed off it.

". . . as Adam tilled the soil, watering it with the sweat of his brow, bearing the first fruits of his labor under your guiding hand . . ."

I groaned with Dad. The Reverend was starting with Genesis. That was bad. That was really bad.

Whenever the Reverend Carstairs prayed, he picked a point in the Bible and traced it all the way through to Revelation. He liked to end with all the heathen being thrown into the lake of fire. It wasn't bad—it wasn't *too* bad—when he began somewhere in the New Testament, but starting with Genesis could take hours.

". . . as Abraham offered his son Isaac to you upon the altar, and as you gave him the ram in the thicket . . ."

"I hate prayers," Grampa mumbled.

"Hush, dear." Gramma nudged him in the ribs with her elbow, none too gently.

". . . and David, a man after your own heart . . ."

What seemed like a ba-zillion hours went by, and still the Reverend prayed. There was a lot less steam on the potatoes than when the prayer had started. Everybody still had their heads bowed, but I knew nobody could be *that* thankful.

". . . and Amminadab begat Nahshon, and Nahshon begat Salmon . . ."

The Reverend went on and on and on, and then on and on some more. Finally, when he *had* to know everything was cold, he said, "And be with us now, and forevermore, and protect us from the wrath of your justice, and throw us not into the fiery pits of Hell, where there is wailing and gnashing of teeth. Amen, and amen.

"Pass the potatoes," he said as he sat down.

The food was a little cold, but it wasn't too bad. We had turkey, stuffing, cranberries, potatoes, rolls, sweet potatoes, you name it, we had it. I took extra turkey because I like turkey.

Grampa and Dad talked about the weather and the Vikings. Gramma and Mom just talked. Me and Jackey ate and listened and answered questions when we were asked. The Reverend Carstairs didn't talk to anybody. He just ate. Eating and praying and slapping microphones were the only three things he knew how to do.

"Good potatoes, Mom," Jackey said.

"Thank you."

"I like the stuffing."

Mom glared at Gramma but didn't say anything.

We ate and ate and ate some more. Finally I only had room left inside for pie, and it would have to be shoved in the cracks. We all stopped, except the Reverend. He didn't stop until there wasn't any food left on the table.

Mom took our orders, pumpkin or apple, then went into the kitchen. Gramma followed. The Reverend slid his chair back and searched the table for any scraps he might have missed.

"Do you follow football, Reverend?" Grampa asked.

"Football is such a worldly game," the Reverend

said, "and God's holy word says to be ye in the world, but not of it."

Reverend Carstairs was definitely not of the world. He was from another planet.

"Baseball, on the other hand," the Reverend continued, "is a divine thing. The parallel between the pitcher and batter to the Holy Word can only be accounted for by divine inspiration. Praise God for baseball! Praise Him!"

Grampa stared at the Reverend for a moment, then stood. "I'll take my pie in the living room, Abby." He walked away, shaking his head. Me and Jackey and Dad followed. The Reverend didn't seem to notice we were gone.

Mom brought us our pie with a scoop of vanilla ice cream on the side. As soon as the Reverend's was gone, he stood up.

"I must be going, Abby," he said. "Thank you for the dinner."

"Already?"

"Don't hold him up, Abby," Grampa muttered. "Shovel him out the door."

"Hush, dear." Gramma gave him a shot in the ribs again.

"I'm afraid so," the Reverend said. "There are other members of the flock in need of tending. Good-bye, dear, and good-bye to you, Jack. Thomas, do your Sunday-school lessons. My granddaughter tells me you haven't been doing your lessons."

"Yes sir." I *hate* Marietta.

As soon as the door closed behind the Reverend, Grampa raised his leg and farted.

"August!" Gramma stared at him.

"Been waiting to do that ever since he walked in the door," Grampa said. "Preachers give me gas."

Gramma clicked her tongue and went in to help Mom with the dishes. Us "men" sat in the living room and burped and farted.

Grampa stuffed tobacco in his pipe bowl. "So what's going on out here, Jack?" he asked. "Everything looks so much more . . . run down than when I lived here."

"Things are older, Dad."

"When things get old, you either fix them or replace them. You don't let them fall down around your ears."

"Things aren't exactly falling down around my ears. Times are hard. I'm working another job. Something's got to give for a little while, until I get back on my feet."

"Well, not my farm. Let something else give, as you put it."

"Dad—"

"There's nothing wrong out here that a little hard work couldn't fix. You're just being lazy, Jack." Grampa lit his pipe and started puffing. Dad watched him but didn't say anything.

After a while, Jackey and Grampa fell asleep and Dad turned on the football game. The Vikings were getting their butts kicked. It was only the beginning of the second quarter and the score was already twenty-three to zip. On their own five-yard line, the Vikings' quarterback flubbed an easy pass, throwing an interception instead. Normally when that happened, Dad swore and buried his face in his hands. This time he just stared.

I went up to my room. I lay down and listened to Gramma's and Mom's muffled voices drift up from the kitchen. Grampa snored. Pretty soon I was sleeping, too.

CHAPTER NINE

Christmas came the same time it always did, but we hardly noticed. Santa Claus was getting pretty stingy. He brought me a pair of pants. Grampa and Gramma Morrell gave me a game, and Grampa and Gramma Tinsdale sent me a watch from Georgia. Jackey got about the same. Mom and Dad didn't get anything. Ho, ho, ho.

Two days after Christmas, it snowed four inches. We were still on our school vacation (I call it the winter prisoner-release program), so as soon as the sun came up and we'd finished a breakfast that would last us all day, me and Jackey went out to pack the snow down on the sledding hill. We used mini boggans, sheets of colored plastic, to slide on. We couldn't use sleds with runners on the hill, because they tore up the grass, and with the sledding games we played, it was dangerous having all that metal around.

Along about ten in the morning, Kelly came over with a mini boggan.

"Is it ready?" she asked.

"It's ready," I said. Jackey nodded.

She walked down the hill, examining it, then came back up again. "This is the first good snow of the year. Does everybody remember the rules?"

We remembered the rules. We recited them every year before the first run. Here they are:

1. Never walk up the sliding lanes. If you do, you have to fix the holes you make.
2. Never spit on the lanes.
3. If you have to leave for lunch, you're a pussy, and you have to put up with being called one for the rest of the day.
4. If you cry, you're a pussy. For the rest of this rule, see rule number three.
5. If you leave before sunset, you're a pussy. For the rest of this rule, see rule number four, which will refer you to rule number three.

As soon as everyone had them straight, we got down to business.

We knew every sledding game you can think of, and probably a ba-zillion you can't. We played tag on sleds and army and king of the hill. We raced each other and had distance runs. We had one game that we couldn't think of a good name for. Two of us got on the same sled at the same time and fought all the way down. The winner was the one who stayed on longest. Kelly usually won because she fought dirty. I only beat her once all day. She jumped off the sled. I couldn't figure out why until I crashed into a tree.

You can fly on a sled, and hitting a tree going a million miles an hour is no picnic. I konked my head and twisted my arm and woke up the next morning with a black eye the size of a beach ball. None of that was important. The important thing was I beat Kelly.

We stayed outside all day, just like the rules say. Mom came out around lunchtime, but she left us alone. Mom didn't know the rules because she grew up in Georgia, where everybody's a pussy. Dad knew the rules and never bothered us on a good sledding day. Usually parents are pretty good about letting you stay on the hill; after all, parents were kids once. Most of them, anyway.

Around four o'clock it started getting dark, and by five a person couldn't see a snowball if someone threw it right square in his face. I knew because I tried it on Jackey.

The game we played after dark was what the rest of the day led up to. It was the cream of the cream of the cream of sledding games. It required perfect blackness, ultimate courage, and a really thick head.

The game we played after dark was called Kill the Turd.

In Kill the Turd one person (usually Jackey because he was the smallest) became the turd and had to slide to the bottom of the hill. Once he got there, the rules of the game said that no matter what happened, he couldn't move. Me and Kelly went down after him, aiming in the darkness for where we thought the turd might be. If we hit the turd, we got to go back up the hill and try to hit it again. If we missed the turd, we became the turd. You can see why we had to play at night. Collisions are always better when you can't see them coming.

We'd been playing Kill the Turd for about an hour. Kelly had been at the bottom for quite a while; I must have crashed into her at least five times just myself. It was my turn again.

"Here I come, you turd!"

"All right."

And down I went. I buried my face in the plastic to decrease wind resistance, but I forgot about my feet. My left one dragged. That threw my course off. I tried to correct for it, but I couldn't see her in the darkness, and by the time I was close enough to, so much snow was flying into my face it didn't make any difference. I sailed right by her. I rolled off my sled and stayed where I stopped.

"Tom's the turd!" Kelly called.

"Are you the turd, Tom?"

"Yeah," I yelled. "I'm the turd."

Kelly laughed and ran back up the hill. I've never seen anyone so lucky. I'd been going a ba-zillion times the speed of sound, and if I'd stayed on course I would've *mangled* her. I learned my lesson. *Never* drag your feet.

As soon as she was out of sight, the yard lights at the house came on. That was Mom's signal to come in. It was still too dark for the guys to see me.

"Last run," I shouted.

"All right," Kelly shouted back.

I hated being the turd on the last run. That meant both would come down at once, and if they hit me, pretty near every bone in my body would break. But what could I do? Turd rules said I couldn't move.

Things were really quiet for about thirty seconds. Then this chanting started at the top of the hill, real soft at first, but growing louder all the time.

"Kill the turd, kill the turd, kill the turd . . ."

I heard them coming long before I saw them. The raspy scratch of plastic on snow grew louder and louder. My heart pounded so hard it echoed.

The moon came out from behind a cloud, lighting the hill up silver. I saw Jackey first, speeding toward me like a bowling ball, right on target. Kelly was right behind him. I put my head down. They were going to hit me, and it was going to hurt. It was going to hurt bad. I closed my eyes and prayed.

"Please God, make them miss. Hit them with a lightning bolt or something. If you do, I'll never do anything wrong again."

I looked up. They were still coming. Obviously God didn't believe me. I'd have to sound more like Jesus, more divine, and I'd have to do it fast.

"Heavenly Father, if it's possible for this cup to pass from me, let it pass. Give it to one of them. Give it—"

That's as far as I got. I drank the cup.

Jackey plowed into me low and I flipped over his back. My boots came down and caught Kelly right on the chin, but not hard enough to stop her. The top of her head hit me in the stomach like a cannonball. Just as I doubled over, Jackey's boots whipped around and smashed me in the face.

When I came to, we were all lying in a pile. Nobody dared move for fear of broken bones. Nobody laughed or said anything; we just groaned. It wasn't fun until the initial pain wore off.

Jackey was the first to speak. "That was a good one."

"Yeah. I kicked Kelly right in the chin."

Kelly checked her jaw with both hands. It was still in one piece, so she tried to use it. "At least I got you worse than you got me."

"Did not."

"Did so!"

"Well," Jackey broke in, "I killed the turd worse than you did, Kelly."

"Yeah?"

"Yeah."

"Did not!"

"Did so!"

The lights at the house flicked off and back on again.

"We have to go, guys," I said.

"All right." Nobody moved. We still didn't know if we could stand.

I was the first one to try, and after staggering for a second I was all right. The only thing wrong with me was my eye and what felt like a couple of shattered ribs. The other two climbed groaning to their feet. We stood in the moonlight and stared at each other.

"You coming over tomorrow?" Jackey asked.

"Yeah," Kelly said. "I'll bring the wooden toboggan. We'll see how the turd does against that." I knew she was kidding. Someone could get hurt playing Kill the Turd with a wooden toboggan.

After the collision, Kelly's sled had skittered farther down the hill, and when she tried to retrieve it, she limped. I got it for her.

"Thanks," she said when I handed it back. She smiled.

The moon shone high and bright on her face. Her teeth flashed and her hair poked out from under her stocking cap, framing her face. Two moons reflected in her eyes. When she smiled, they smiled. My heart fluttered like it had never fluttered before.

Wow.

I tell you what, time stopped, because in the ten seconds I stood staring at her, two hours passed. Kelly was the most beautiful girl I'd ever seen. I mean, she was *beautiful*.

"See you tomorrow," she said.

Listening to her was like listening to birds singing. It was like hearing water tumble down a waterfall or the low, soft burp a frog makes right after it swallows a bug. I'd heard her voice a ba-zillion times and I'd never noticed before how beautiful it was. I didn't answer her. I couldn't. I just stood there like a dummy.

"Tom?"

"Huh?" Oh, real witty, the perfect thing to say. I can see a famous international spy meeting a beautiful woman and saying, "Huh?"

"Are you all right?"

"Yeah." Huh and yeah. Maybe I could throw in a "gee" and really impress her.

"So I'll see you tomorrow."

"Uh-huh."

She smiled again. Two dimples appeared in her cheeks. My legs got all woozy. I thought I was going to collapse.

She trotted off through First Woods like a fairy

princess dancing in the moonlight. I just stood there and watched her.

"Are you coming?" Jackey asked. I'd forgotten he was there. "Tom?"

"Huh?"

"What's the matter with you?"

I didn't know.

"Are you coming?" he asked again.

"Yeah." I followed him to the house.

Kelly was a girl. I know that sounds obvious, but I'd never thought of her as one before. She had always been just one of the guys, but she wasn't, she wasn't at all. She was a girl.

Kelly was a girl.

Gee.

We had to take our snow clothes off in the basement, because as soon as the snow melted, they'd be soaking wet. Sometimes they weren't the only things that get soaking wet after a day on the hill.

In the cold, you hardly notice when your bladder fills up. That's because your whole system freezes. The first thing that thaws when you come back into the house is the "you better go pee" nerve, and it thaws in a hurry.

"Help me, Tom." Jackey hopped up and down. He had his hat and coat off, but was having trouble grabbing his pants zipper. Don't laugh. When your fingers are numb, you have trouble grabbing a basketball.

"You'll never make it," I said. "You've got two more pairs of pants on under those."

"That's why you have to help me."

"What do you want me to do?" I was doing a pretty good dance myself. My fingers felt ten feet thick. I couldn't even *find* my zipper.

Jackey pushed his thumbs together on each side of the zipper tongue. He bent way over, still hopping, and groaned with the effort of pulling it down. He got it halfway before it stopped. He ran a quick lap around the furnace, then looked at me again, like one of those starving kids on the foster-child posters.

"You want me to get Mom?"

"No." Of course not. It's embarrassing to have your mom pull your pants down for you.

"Come over here." We skipped over to a heating duct running out of the furnace. "Hold your hands over this until they thaw out a bit."

"That'll take too long!"

"What else can we do?"

We hopped up and down with our hands over the duct, feeling miserable. Every once in a while we took a lap. The only sounds we made were occasional pathetic grunts and the slap of our feet on the floor. If we'd been wearing tap shoes and a talent scout had seen us, we'd be famous by now. The Bladder Brothers.

It wasn't long before I felt a tingling like a thousand tiny needles pricking my fingertips. I tried my zipper, but it was still no go. I felt a little trickle in my underwear and had to clamp down hard.

"Waterfalls," I said, "rushing, gushing waterfalls pouring in warm, wet streams over the cliff. Leaky faucets, drip, drip, dripping—"

"Shut up, Tom!"

If I was going to pee in my pants, I was going to do everything I could to keep from being the only person who did.

"Rushing rivers, mighty torrents—"

Jackey punched me. Low. In the bladder.

I had to take three quick laps and pinch it off with both hands before I got myself under control.

"Don't do that!"

"Then shut up!" We both danced again.

Jackey's fingers were littler, so they thawed quicker. He had his pants off and was running up the stairs before I could even work my zipper.

"Firehoses," I yelled after him, "dousing a great porcelain bowl! Big glasses of spilled lemonade!"

It didn't work. I heard the entryway bathroom door slam shut, his feet pounding like a herd of rampaging buffalo, then the sound of captive urine being set free. That made me *really* have to go.

Finally, I got my pants off and sprinted up the stairs, or came as close to sprinting as I dared. Mom and Dad were in the kitchen. The supper was on the table. I ran past it and them on my tippy-toes with both hands clutched between my legs. They stared at me with the most ridiculous expressions you've ever seen.

I made it up the stairs and into the bathroom and almost got my underwear down before instinct took over.

So close, but yet so far. I'd have to change before I went down to dinner.

I tell you what, God's a pretty neat guy. He could have made peeing painful, but He didn't.

After a whole day of sledding, peeing is the most wonderful feeling in the world.

CHAPTER TEN

I like winter and I like spring, but I don't like what's between them. God scraped the scum off the other seasons and threw it in right after winter. The muck season. Spring, Summer, Fall, Winter, and Muck.

During Muck, the world is ice cream God left sitting out too long. Snow turns to slush. Dirt turns to mud. The pig manure me and Dad spent the winter shoveling out of the barn turned to God-knows-what-I-don't-even-want-to-think-about-it. And everything is dirty gray. Even the sky.

We checked the brooder house's warming lamps, then set up the cardboard inside. Just as Muck was getting over, we ordered our chicks. We bought the same number as the year before, thirty sexed female and twenty straight run. Two were pecked to death before we could get tar on their wounds.

And then the planting started. Until it was over, there was work like you couldn't begin to believe. Plowing and disking and fertilizing and planting and cultivating, from the time the sun came up until the time it went down again, and sometimes even after that. The farmers went to work in the morning as eager as little kids. When they came in at lunch, they were still young and able to laugh and smile, but by suppertime they hunched over their meals silently, like old men. When night came, they collapsed in their beds as stone dead as corpses. The next day, they did it all over again. They lived whole lives every single day.

All that farmwork and Dad still worked nights at Mercer's. I don't think he slept more than three hours any one day, and for two days straight he didn't sleep at all. By the time the planting was done, he looked older than Grampa.

But he wasn't quiet and moody like he had been the year before. He was happy. He sang in the fields, he sang while he ate, he sang before he went to work at Mercer's. When you put seed in the ground, you put hope in with it, and hope always makes a person happy.

We planted soybeans again. Don't ask me why; after last year's disaster, I sure wouldn't have. I asked Dad about it.

"Because," he said, "we used up all our bad luck on beans last year."

Some reason. From what I've seen, farmers always have enough bad luck to last two years in a row.

We finished planting on a Saturday afternoon, and as Dad drove the tractor up the driveway, big, dark thunderheads crawled over the western horizon. The whole family sat on the porch and watched them come in. Thunder muttered under the clouds' breath, and when the first big drops fell, Dad put his arm around Mom's shoulder and kissed her.

We ate supper on the porch, then Dad went to bed; he was lucky enough to get overtime at Mercer's. Me and Mom and Jackey sat out there for hours, listening to the thunder and watching the lightning crisscross the sky. It was still raining when we went to bed. I left the bedroom window open and watched the breeze lift the curtain. The air smelled wet and good and black, like I knew Dad wanted it to smell. The drops sounded like a lullaby on the roof, and the thunder rolled, liked Dad's singing, gently over the fields. I hadn't slept so good in a long, long time.

When Dad came in the next morning, he walked right past his breakfast out to the porch. I followed him.

"The forecasters are wrong," he said as he stared across the fields. "It's going to be a good year."

"I think so, too."

"Where's your mother?"

"Still in bed."

115

"Good." He strutted into the bedroom like a rooster into a henhouse. A moment later, Mom giggled. I went back to my breakfast.

"Where's Dad?" Jackey asked.

"In the bedroom. He's pretty tired."

Something banged against the wall. Mom giggled again.

"It doesn't sound like he's tired," Jackey said. "What are they doing?"

"I don't know."

"What's Mom laughing about?"

"Dad must be telling her a joke." What was I supposed to say? It wasn't *my* job to tell him that stuff.

"Must be a good joke," he said.

"Must be."

When the first bean shoots came up, Mom took one of the butchered chickens out of the freezer and fixed it just like a turkey. We had a feast and a little party on the porch afterward. Dad took out his guitar. Mom sang that she'd be comin' 'round the mountain when she came, and Dad left the Red River Valley, and me and Jackey trudged into the kitchen to tell Aunt Rhodie that the old gray goose was dead. We laughed and sang some more and Mom made popcorn and we had a good old time until Dad broke one of his guitar strings. After that we played Parcheesi. The only interruption we had in three games was around eight o'clock, when it started raining again. It was the best time I'd had in ten ba-zillion years. No lie.

And then the rain stopped.

When I woke up the next morning, the sky was blue and pretty and the sun was hot. The next day was the same, and so was the day after that. Those pretty blue days just kept coming, piling on top of each other like the last run of Kill the Turd. The black soil turned gray and the mist turned to dust and the sky was just as blue and the sun was just as hot, but it wasn't pretty anymore. It wasn't pretty at all.

One morning, Dad came in from work. Just like before, he skipped his breakfast and went out on the porch. This time he kept going. He walked down the driveway and across the road into Little Crow's field. I followed him, staying back so he wouldn't hear me.

He knelt at the field's edge and picked up a dirt clod. He rolled it gently between his fingers. As it crumbled, the breeze carried the dust away.

"Maybe it'll come yet," he said. "Maybe." His head dropped and his shoulders shook. His breath whistled in his throat; then he covered his face with his hands and cried. He crouched in the dust, crying, and I stood behind him, not knowing what to do. I'd never seen my dad cry before.

He wiped his face off and stood. When he turned

around, his eyes were wet. Black ink ran down each side of his nose, like dark tears. He tried to smile, but he couldn't smile. He walked back to me and put his hand on my shoulder.

"I'm trying, son," he said. "I'm giving it my best. You know that, don't you?"

"Sure, Dad. I know that."

He hugged me to his chest so I couldn't see his face. He cried again, his rough palm trembling as it pressed against my cheek. Then he let me go. He walked back to the house.

I stood in the field and watched him go. I started crying myself. I was thirteen and there I was, bawling like a baby. I knew it was silly, but I couldn't make myself stop.

I looked at the ground. My tears fell onto the soil. For a second they left little black circles, and then the dust sucked the circles gray again. It looked like no tears had fallen there at all.

CHAPTER ELEVEN

Mom quit working at the nursing home. "I need more time to pray," she explained.

"Praying doesn't bring in a paycheck," Dad told her.

"God will provide."

Mom opened one of the second-floor spare bedrooms up, the same one she hid out in when Aunt Maggie died. She put in a bed and a lamp and a big picture of Jesus she'd taken out of their room downstairs. She called it her prayer closet.

Dad spent all his time on the porch, studying the fields, his big hands caressing a beer bottle taken from the cooler he always kept at his side. From a distance he looked about the same as he did any other year, and watching him made me think that nothing had changed, but up close I knew everything had. Bags hung under his eyes now, and the whites were all dried out, like chalk dust. It made me feel funny, looking at him. I didn't know if I should feel sorry or be afraid.

After supper one night, Mom went up to her prayer closet. Dad filled his cooler and sat on the porch. Me and Jackey went out to fix the gate on Chester's cage. Cleo had taken to knocking it in—she couldn't stand Chester eating in peace.

"I'm going to kill Cleo," Jackey said.

"You're not going to touch Cleo."

"I have to. If I don't, she'll kill Chester."

"No she won't." She might, but if she did, would that be such a bad thing?

"How do you know?"

"Because if she was going to, she'd have done it by now. Chester's always been able to get away."

"So far she has, anyway," Jackey said.

"Will you forget about the chicken? I want to get this done." I clamped down on the gate with a pliers. "By the way, we have to walk beans tomorrow."

"I don't wanna walk beans."

La-di-da. As if that was going to get him out of it. "I don't care if you want to or not. Dad's working too much to do it, and Mom's in bed. I can't walk them all myself."

"I'll tell Dad if you make me help."

"I already talked to him. He said you have to help me."

"Get Kelly to."

120

"We can't afford to pay her."

"Aw." He went back to work. I could tell he was out of arguments.

So the next day, me and Jackey walked beans.

I had to show him *everything*. I've never seen anyone so dumb. He didn't even know what a *ragweed* looks like. How can you not know what a ragweed looks like?

We spent the whole day in Little Crow's field. There wasn't a cloud in sight—the sky looked like someone had paint rollered it blue. The heat whistled like pain in my ears. The air was so dry it crackled.

"Why do we have to do this?" Jackey asked.

"I already told you why." I wasn't in any mood for talking.

"I don't wanna be out here," he whined. He'd been whining ever since we started. I was sick and tired of listening to him.

"Get that ragweed by your foot."

"My hands hurt," he griped.

"So do mine."

"I'm thirsty."

"I am, too."

We started up the hill, heading west. The sun was straight overhead. My legs felt like I'd been taking laps up and down the stairs in the Empire State Building. Jackey stumbled along behind me, using his hoe the same way Grampa used his cane.

"Who cares about the darn old beans anyway?" he asked.

He had me there. I sure didn't.

We trudged along, pulling a ragweed or cockleburr every few feet. The sweat stung my eyes, making them tear. Everything looked vague and watery, like I was seeing things through a dream.

"I'm thirsty," Jackey whined. "Why are we doing this, anyway?"

I ignored him. The next cockleburr I pulled I imagined to be his head. It ripped out of his shoulders, roots and all.

"Beans, shmeens, teens, jeans. Boy oh boy do I hate beans." Jackey lifted his hoe and pretended to shoot a crow flying overhead. He walked right past an elephant ear.

That's what did it. That's what broke it loose.

I knocked the hoe out of his hands and slapped him, hard. A big red mark jumped out of his face. He looked at me with his hands up in the air as if he was still holding the hoe, too shocked to move, too shocked to even cry.

"Listen, you spoiled little brat, I'm sick to death of listening to your whining! Shut your mouth and pull the weeds or I'll slap your face again!"

Jackey just stared at me. Tears welled up in his eyes. He picked up his hoe, then dropped it and walked across the rows toward the house.

122

"Where are you going?"

He never said a word.

"All right, run home to Mom, you little sissy! You little Mama's boy!"

But he just kept walking, right across the road and up the drive and into the house. He didn't come out again.

Fine. If that's the way he wanted to be, fine. I'd rather work without him.

It was almost six o'clock when I finally went back to the house. A crow cawed at me as I crossed the yard. I knew somebody else would be cawing as soon as I stepped inside.

"Thomas?" Mom's voice dropped down the stairs like a bowling ball. "Will you come up here, please?"

When I went through the kitchen, Dad was taking beer and ice out of the refrigerator and putting them in his cooler. "You missed your supper," he said.

"I was working."

"How'd it go?"

I stopped in the stairwell. "I can only do so much working alone, Dad."

"Wasn't Jackey helping you?"

"Part of the day. He's worthless."

"He's just a kid, Tom."

I didn't say anything. Sometimes I wished I was

just a kid, too. Sometimes I wished all I had to do was play and color pictures for my Sunday-school lesson and read comic books. But that wasn't the way things were. Not for me. And not for Jackey anymore, either.

"Boys should be boys," Mom had said, "for as long as they can."

Dad pointed with a beer neck up the stairs. "You better see what your mother wants. Supper's warming in the oven when you're done."

A stiff, stale smell hung in the prayer closet, like something had died a long time ago and never been taken away. The lamp was on and all the curtains drawn. Mom sat on the bed with her big Bible squatting like a toad in her lap. Her face was pale and her lips were pasty and all the color was out of her hair. She looked like she'd been leeched.

"Thomas," she asked, "what happened with John, Jr., today?"

"Nothing."

"Don't lie to me. If you lie to me, you lie to God, and God can see into your heart. Do you know what happens to liars after they die?"

I knew, but didn't answer. I tried to think of what Clint would say.

"They go to Hell," Mom said. "Liars go to Hell."

"Nothing happened, Mom." What did I have to lose? I'd been lying on and off to one person or another for as long as I could remember. If lying sent me to Hell, I was already beyond hope. One more lie on top of the pile wasn't going to make any difference. It's probably that way with most people.

Mom set her Bible alongside her leg. "Come here, Thomas." I came. "Kneel."

"Aw, Mom—"

"I said kneel!" She came at me with her hands like claws and a snarl pulling at the corners of her lips. She grabbed the back of my neck and jerked me down. She was a wild thing as withered as death but neither dead or alive, like a demon, like a ghoul. If I'd just walked in and seen her that way, I wouldn't have known who she was, I swear to God, I wouldn't have known who she was. I was so scared I almost hit her, and that scared me even more.

She dug her nails into my neck and held my head so I had to look at the wall. "What do you see?" Her voice was as sharp as her nails. I was too scared to know what I was supposed to say.

"What do you see!"

"Jesus, Mom." Jesus' picture hung on the wall. He had big brown eyes and snow-white skin and a glow around him. The crown of thorns dug into his fore-head.

"And what does Jesus do to sinners?"

"He forgives them, Mom."

She shook my head so hard, it looked like Jesus would leap right off the wall. I closed my eyes and

125

prayed to Him to take me away.

"What does he do to unsaved sinners?"

"He throws them in Hell. Is that what you want to hear? He throws them in Hell." I stared at the picture.

I took my prayer back. I took every prayer I'd ever made back. Jesus, savior of the world, creator of Hell, torturer of souls. I hated him. On behalf of all the sinners and all the Muslims and Buddhists and Hindus and Catholics and Jews, I hated him. Jesus, I thought, I'll never pray to you again.

"And what are you?" Mom asked.

I didn't say anything. I glared at Jesus.

"Answer me!"

"I'm a sinner, Mom, and I'm going to burn in Hell! All right?"

With her other hand, she pulled my head to her chest. The stiff, stale smell clung to her like the smell of vomit. It oozed from her pores.

"Yes," she said, "you are a sinner. But you're not going to burn in Hell. Not my boy. With Jesus' grace, we're going to take care of that right now."

She bent me over until my face was buried in the mattress. "Now pray after me," she said.

"Mom—"

"Do it!" Her fingernails trembled on my neck. They cut skin.

"Oh God," she cried, "look down on me, a sinner."

I didn't say anything. She pushed my face farther into the mattress. I could hardly breathe.

"Oh God, look down on me, a sinner," she repeated.

"Oh God, look down on me, a sinner." But I wasn't praying.

"And forgive my errant ways." Her nails felt like teeth searching for my throat.

"And forgive my errant ways."

"And save my soul from the fires of Hell."

"And save my soul from the fires of Hell."

She let go of me then, and when I looked up, tears were coursing down her face. She smiled. She had the same watery, blind look the Reverend Carstairs always had.

"Look at Jesus," she said. "He's the one who saved you. He's the one who set you free."

Blood ran down Jesus' forehead from the thorns that pierced his skin. It ran down the bridge of his nose and around his eyes like tears as He watched my mother.

"Praise Him!" she shouted.

"I praise him." The monster. The killer. I watched him cry.

"Yes, praise Him! Glory to God!" Mom lifted her hands, then picked up her Bible and held it to her chest. She closed her eyes and smiled to no one at all. "My boy is saved," she whispered. "Bless God."

I still knelt beside the bed. I wanted to leave but didn't know if I should. I didn't want her going crazy again.

Finally, Mom opened her eyes. "You can go now, my son, my new lamb of God." When she ran her hand through my hair, I flinched.

I stood. I didn't look at her. As I walked by Jesus, I saw a thin coating of dust over his face. Mom couldn't see it from where she was.

"Read the third chapter of John tonight," she said. "And pray. Pray to God for His blessing and protection. He provides for His lambs."

I left without answering her. She started blessing God again.

I walked out of the house and into the pasture. I followed the creek through First Woods until it turned south and crossed under the road. Normally on my walks, I headed back to the house from there, but not that night. I kept walking because when I walked I didn't have to think and I didn't have to remember, I didn't have to do anything but walk. When I looked up to see where I was, the sun had set and the stars were out. I forgot all about my supper.

Jesus and Mom. Good Lord.

It took a long time before I realized I was crying. I'd never hated either of them before.

CHAPTER TWELVE

Every Thursday night that summer, the Reverend Carstairs came out to the house. He and Mom raised a cry unto the Lord together up in the prayer closet. It sounded like a cat fight.

The crop failed. Dad just plowed it under. He worked overtime at Mercer's every chance he got.

"If we're going to make the payments this fall, I'll have to bring extra money in," he said one morning at breakfast. "I'm happy to get the hours."

"You hate it, don't you?" Instead of answering me, he went out to the porch to watch the wind blow over the empty fields. That was answer enough.

Mom purged the house. That's what she called throwing out everything that had even the most remote connection to sin. In other words, everything good.

"God provides for His children," she said, "and if He is to provide for us, we need to start acting like His children."

She even threw out some of Jackey's comic books. "The big-busted women they draw on every page are enticements of the flesh."

"Mom," I said, "Jackey doesn't even know what an enticement is."

She got thin lipped and shook her head. "I won't have my boys straying from the straight and narrow. I don't care where the temptation comes from." So we couldn't watch TV unless she approved it first. We couldn't even listen to the radio unless it was one of those corny religious programs.

"It's just a phase," Dad said. "She'll get over it." I wondered if sitting on the porch half drunk was just a phase, too. I wondered if Kelly was. It had been six months since I'd fallen in love with her, and I still treated her like one of the guys.

One afternoon, me and Kelly were sitting on the fence by the pasture, doing nothing. I wasn't *trying* to do nothing, but that's what it had turned into. The moment wasn't right to ask her out. The moment was never right—either it was raining or it was the wrong day of the week or I had a sore throat. It's a wonder anyone ever goes out at all.

The back door slammed. Dad came out with his work clothes on: a button-down shirt with the

sleeves cut off and a stained pair of blue jeans. He'd
gotten overtime and was going in to work early. He
climbed in his pickup and drove down the driveway.
When we waved, he ignored us.

"What's the matter with your old man lately?"
Kelly asked.

"Nothing."

"He's always grumpy."

"He worries a lot."

"About what?"

"I don't know." I did, but I didn't want to tell her.
I'd seen the letters from the Farmers Home Administration and the bank piling up. I knew what they
were; I'm no ignorant.

I watched Kelly out of the corner of my eye, trying to ogle her without looking like too much of a
goof. Her skin was tanned dark and her hair was short
and brown and she was *so* pretty. She ranked right up
there with Mrs. Kramer. Of course, she didn't have
the body Mrs. Kramer had. Not yet, anyway.

We stood there for a long time without saying
anything. She was *so* pretty. I wondered what a date
with her would be like. Lousy. I didn't have any of
the right things for a really good date, the kind of
date that would impress her. I didn't have a Porsche
or a private jet. I'd never been to Paris, so I didn't
know any of the good restaurants, but that didn't
make any difference because I didn't have the ba-

zillion dollars it must cost for plane tickets to fly there. Everything was stacked against me. The best I could do was a lousy movie. Big deal.

"I ought to be going," she said. "It's almost suppertime." The wind lifted her hair as she jumped off the fence. She was *so* pretty.

I couldn't wait any longer. If I didn't ask her out right then, right at that very moment, I'd go bonkers.

"'Bye," she said.

"'Bye."

She walked across the pasture toward First Woods. I stood and watched her like a dummy.

All right, if you're going to do it, then do it. Just quit thinking about it. Quit being such a clod.

She disappeared into the trees.

"Damn it." I looked around real quick, but Mom was nowhere in sight. Good. If she tried to make me pray again, I didn't know what I'd do.

After supper, me and Jackey went outside to do the chores. I was watching the hogs pig out when Jackey flew through the door. His eyes were big. He was too frightened to speak.

"What's the matter?"

"Chester . . ." He stared at me, wild eyed, then disappeared back outside. I followed him.

Jackey was standing by the cage with Chester cuddled to his chest. "Cleo almost killed her," he said. "She tore the gate open while Chester was inside. Chester didn't have anywhere to run."

She didn't look too bad, not much worse than usual, anyway. She had a gash in her shoulder, but that was about it. She'd been lucky.

"I'll get the tar," I said. Jackey murmured to the chicken. Chester trembled in his arms, too frightened to move.

Stupid bird. I wouldn't have had all that trouble if Jackey had just picked a real chicken for a pet. No, he had to pick the scrawniest, ugliest little runt there was. Any chicken that required the special attention Jackey gave Chester didn't deserve to live. That's how I saw it, anyway.

I dabbed tar on the gash. "She'll be all right."

Jackey hugged her to his chest again. The bird didn't move. "So what can I do?"

"About what?"

"About keeping Chester safe?"

"I know one thing you can't do. You can't feed her separately anymore. If Cleo catches her in the pen again, she'll kill her."

"Chester will get sick and scrawny."

"Yeah." As if she hadn't always been. "But at least she'll be alive."

Jackey scratched Chester's neck. The stupid thing cowered like a mongrel about to be hit.

"Go talk to Cleo," Jackey said.

"What?"

"Tell her to leave Chester alone. Tell her that if

133

she doesn't, she'll be the first one to lose her head this fall."

"What the—"

"Tell her!"

I shrugged. "All right." I walked over to the trees, where Cleo roosted. "You have to leave Chester alone," I said, feeling like an idiot. Cleo clucked once, then preened her feathers. She ignored me.

"I said you have to leave Chester alone. Do you hear me?"

Jesus Criminey, what did I expect, an answer? I reached up and scratched her, then walked back to the pen.

Jackey set Chester down. She ran and hid under the shed corner.

"Did she listen?" he asked.

"How do I know? She's a chicken."

He grunted. "You're not much if you can't make your own chicken listen to you." He huffed away into the house.

I didn't answer him. What was I supposed to say?

I tell you what, I couldn't do anything that night. I tried watching TV and I couldn't. I tried reading and I couldn't. Everything I tried, I couldn't do. I had Kelly on the brain. It had been almost three whole hours since I'd last seen her, and like a junkie, I was going through withdrawals. So along about sunset, I headed off across the pasture toward her house.

I spent half the night standing in front of the Tohreys' living-room window. It was dark enough so I could see in without them seeing out. And what luck! Kelly was modeling dresses. She'd come in with one on and turn in a circle in front of Ello and Lois, and they'd nod and say something I couldn't hear, then she'd leave and come back a few minutes later with a different one. She modeled I bet ten times, and she was *so* pretty. My favorite dress was a shimmering green one with slit sleeves she tied with long green straps halfway down her upper arm. She looked so pretty in that dress, my brain froze up.

Kelly wasn't a guy anymore. She was even getting to be more than a girl. You want to know how I knew? She was getting boobs. Just little ones, you understand, but boobs they were.

Jeez, is that something, or what?

It must have been nine o'clock when she finished and sat down to watch TV. From the angle I was at, I couldn't see anything but the top of her head. I watched for another hour. It was worth it, because twice she stood up so I could see her face for a second or two. She was *so* pretty.

Around ten o'clock, she kissed Ello good night and left. The light came on in her room. I thought about climbing a ladder and telling her how much I loved her, but knowing Kelly, she'd have grabbed my balls with one hand and pushed the ladder over with the other. I walked home instead.

When I reached the house, Dad was sitting on the front porch. The light was off. He was drinking out of a big bottle.

"What are you doing home?" I asked.

"Got fired." His voice was heavy and thick. He lifted the bottle to his lips and swallowed. The label shone in the moonlight. Whiskey. I'd never seen Dad drink whiskey before.

"How'd you get fired?"

"I don't know." He sighed. The long white envelopes from the bank and the Farmers Home Administration were scattered around his feet.

"They can't just fire you like that, can they?"

"They can do whatever they want to do." He burped. His breath smelled like poison. "Nice night," he muttered, but he wasn't looking at the darkness. He was looking at the bottle.

I walked around the house and went in the back door. I could have gone in the front, but I didn't want to walk past him. I don't know why. I just didn't.

CHAPTER THIRTEEN

That Sunday, Grampa and Gramma came out for dinner. It was almost like Thanksgiving, with sweet potatoes and corn, but ham instead of turkey. We didn't eat like that often. It was too expensive .

During the meal, Gramma gossiped and Mom preached about Jesus. Grampa tried to talk to Dad about the Vikings, but Dad wasn't in a talking mood. He hadn't been for a while.

After dinner, Mom and Gramma did the dishes. Me and Dad and Grampa and Jackey sat down in front of the tube to watch the football game.

I didn't follow football; neither did Jackey. We just liked to listen to Grampa curse the Vikings, and we'd join him in the pillow bombardment of the television screen when the other team scored a touchdown.

"Those pansies! Those wimps!"

We grinned at each other, then at Grampa. It was only preseason and he *still* cussed. Grampa practiced for the regular season just like the teams did.

By halftime, the dishes were done. Gramma knitted in the rocking chair and Mom curled up on the sofa, reading her Bible. A pillow pile lay on the floor in front of the screen.

"Can I talk to you?" Dad asked Grampa.

Grampa tapped the ash from his pipe bowl into his hand. "Talk to me about what?"

"Why don't we step outside?" Dad stood and waited for Grampa to follow him. He shut the door behind them, but I could hear what they said anyway. I watched them through the window.

"So what do you want to talk to me about?"

"Things are bad this year, Dad. Really bad."

"You lost the crop."

Dad sat down and sighed. "Yeah." He leaned forward with his elbows on his knees, his head down.

"I never lost a crop in my life," Grampa said.

"You never had two years of drought like I've had."

Grampa grunted. "I remember thirty-six. I remember fifty-three. And there were some bad times in the sixties."

"You never choked on loans like I've had to do."

"Bad management," Grampa said.

"Can a third of all farmers be bad managers? Do you think I'm in this alone?"

Grampa grunted again. "The whole time I worked this land, there were farmers going out of business. A few more are going out now than before, and you want to blame it on weather and the government. There's only one place to put the blame—on yourself. Farmers today have grown soft. They've forgotten what it means to work." He sighed. "I thought I raised you better, son."

"Times are hard, Dad."

"I know that, but we're farmers. Times have always been hard." Somewhere out in First Woods a mourning dove cooed, a soft, sad sound, as if it was crying.

"You don't understand what's happening," Dad said. "There's so much up against me."

"I understand more than you think I do. I understand drought. I understand debt. I understand flooding and bugs and blight and dust. I went through it, your granddad went through it, and so did his. We made it. So will you."

"I don't think so."

Grampa packed his pipe. "Just hold on until next year. That's the key. There's always next year."

"Not anymore. Unless I do something drastic, the farm will be gone by then."

"I don't want to hear that. The farm will never be

gone. This is Morrell land."

Dad didn't look up. "I can't help it."

Grampa slammed his fist on the railing. The whole porch vibrated. So did Grampa. "What's the matter with you, boy? You've run my farm into the ground! I look out over my fields and everything's dead! I look at my—"

"No! Do you hear me? No!"

Dad stood up, his fists clenched, the muscles in his forearms and neck knotted tight. "These are *my* fields! This is *my* farm! If it goes down, it'll be me going down, me and my family. My family, *my* wife, *my* children. Not yours!"

Grampa stood quietly by the railing. He looked across the fields, the pipe in his hand forgotten. Gramma still rocked, but her needles stopped knitting. The Bible was open in Mom's lap, but she wasn't looking at it.

Dad sat down and held his face in his hands. When he spoke, his fingers muffled his voice. "You're right about one thing, Dad. Morrell blood flows through these fields. When you touch the soil, I know you feel it, but when they take it away, they'll be taking it away from me, not you."

Grampa didn't say anything.

"You understand that, don't you, Dad?"

Grampa still didn't say anything. He came back into the house, his face tight.

"It's time we headed home, Clare," he said.

"All right, August." Gramma put her knitting away. She followed Grampa to the back door.

Dad stood and leaned his forearms on the railing. He stared over the fields just like Grampa had done, then looked down at his hands. Grampa started his car.

Footsteps came across the kitchen floor. Gramma walked through the living room out onto the porch. She put her arm around Dad's waist, then laid her head on his shoulder. Dad didn't look up, and she didn't say anything.

Grampa honked the horn. Gramma didn't seem to notice. When he honked it a second time, she opened the screen door and climbed down the stairs. She disappeared around the corner of the house.

Grampa and Gramma's car drove away. Dad watched it until the dust plume from its tires settled, then went to the kitchen for a beer.

CHAPTER FOURTEEN

All during supper the next Wednesday, Mom did her best to get our attention, and we did our best to ignore her. She said what she was going to say anyway.

"Tonight we're going to church."

I quit eating. Nothing made me lose my appetite faster than church on a weekday. Besides, me and Jesus weren't on speaking terms.

"We need to show our appreciation to God for all our many blessings," she said.

What blessings?

"I can't," Dad said.

"Why not?"

"Because I have business to attend to." Dad always had business to attend to. During the day, he looked for work or talked to the Farmers Home Administration. I didn't know what he did at night. Maybe some of the banks kept special hours for farmers.

"What business can be more important than God?"

"How about the business of saving the farm?" He threw his napkin down and left the table. Mom didn't say anything. She wasn't about to argue with Dad. The night before, he'd gone out and come home drunk and she had tried. Did they ever rip into each other. Mom accused Dad of being a drunkard. Dad accused Mom of caring more for her Bible than she did for him. I think that maybe they were both right.

"Then the boys and I will go," she said to his empty chair. She picked at her potatoes but didn't eat them.

I kept my mouth shut. It looked like I was going to church. Just like Mom didn't argue with Dad, I didn't argue with her.

People die from Wednesday-night church. They come in, sit down, and never get up again. They get so bored, their brains ooze out of their ears. Doctors have a name for it—well, if they don't, they should. Boredoozioitis, or something like that.

When I went to Wednesday-night church, I always plugged my ears. Mom thought I was trying to keep from listening. That was only partly true—the main reason was I wanted to stay alive.

143

"It is good," Mom said on the way home, "to worship the Lord." Good wasn't the word I was thinking of.

"Hush, Thomas. A minute spent in the Lord's presence is never wasted." I hadn't even said anything.

"Can you drop me off at the Tohreys'?" I asked, just before we reached their house.

"Why?"

"I want to talk to Ello about his tractor."

"I suppose I could." She smiled. "I knew you'd come around. Farming is in the Morrell blood."

"Yeah, maybe."

The last thing I wanted to do was talk to Ello about his tractor. I wanted to see Kelly, but I knew Mom would never drop me off for that. I've learned that if you want to do something you know your parents won't let you do, you have to work interest in your dad's job, homework, or church into it somehow. Try it. It's never failed me.

The shed light was on, so I climbed the fence and went inside. Ello was working on Molly. Kelly sat on the tool bench, swinging her legs back and forth.

"Hiya, Doc."

"Hey, Ello." Kelly was wearing cutoffs and a T-shirt, chewing a piece of bubble gum. She looked just like a model.

"Hey, Kelly."

"Hey."

"What can I help you with?" Ello asked.

"Oh, nothing."

"Kind of late to come over for nothing, isn't it?"

"Kinda." Shoot. If he only knew about me watching Kelly the other night.

Kelly hopped off the bench. Her hair lifted just like it had when she jumped off the fence. She was *so* pretty. "I guess I should be going in. 'Bye."

"'Bye." She looked so good I wanted to puke. When she skipped outside, the moonlight bounced off her hair and showered to the ground like pixie dust. That's what she had to be, a fairy-tale pixie. She was too pretty to be real.

I just watched her go. I was going to blow it again.

"She's getting away," Ello said.

"What?"

He looked up. "You didn't come over to see an old man like me. Go talk to her."

"Actually, I wanted to talk to you about the tractor—"

"Uh-huh." He lumbered to the workbench and picked up a wrench. "I'm not *that* stupid, Doc." He glanced out the shed door, then walked back to the tractor. "If you don't hurry, you'll miss her."

I didn't say anything. How did he know about Kelly? I'd never told anyone how much I loved her before.

"I understand a few things about women, Doc.

You get more accomplished talking to them face to face than you do staring through their living-room windows." He smiled.

Now I knew. I felt like an escaped convict who'd accidentally dug a tunnel into the warden's office.

Kelly was vanishing into the darkness like a fading dream. "You don't mind?" I asked.

"Why would I mind?"

"Thanks, Ello."

"Don't mention it. You better hurry." I cut out of there quicker than a thought.

Man oh man oh man oh man, this was the night, the perfect night. I was going to ask her out. I kid you not. Not even God or the devil was going to stop me.

I caught up with her just before she reached the porch. "Did you forget something?" she asked. She blew a bubble.

"No, I just wanted to talk." Jesus Criminey, I was going to ask her out. The moment was finally right. I was going to *do* it!

We sat on the steps. "So what do you want to talk about?" she asked.

I didn't know how to go about it. "Oh, I don't know." When in doubt, play stupid.

"There must be something."

"Uh . . ." I needed to stall. These things have to be timed just right. The moonlight outlined her face as if with a silver pen. She was *so* pretty.

I was just about to ask her, I mean, I was right there, when disaster struck. The moon went behind a cloud. I could hardly see her. The moment suddenly wasn't right anymore. Perfection was completely ruined.

I collapsed against the steps. I was never going to ask her out. I figured I might as well move away to a convent and become a priest or something.

"Well," she said, "I guess I'll go in. See you tomorrow." She stood up.

"Kelly, wait."

She stopped. "What?"

The perfect moment could take a flying leap at the moon. I'd ask her to the movies now or kill myself. "I . . ."

"What?"

"Uh . . ." My mind went blank. What did I want to ask her?

"Yes?"

"I . . ." Screen. It had something to do with a screen. Screens are at the movies. Movies. Dracula was in the movies. I wanted to suck her neck. That was it.

"Tom, are you all right?"

"I . . ." That couldn't be it. It was something else. It was . . .

"Tom?" She stared at me as if I had a booger hanging out of my nose. "Are you all right?"

"I think so." I did a quick booger check. I was clean. "Yeah."

"Okay. I'll see you tomorrow." She opened the door.

"Kelly, wait." I remembered! "I . . . uh . . . was just wondering if . . . uh . . . maybe you'd like to . . . umm . . . uh . . ."

"Maybe I'd like to what?"

"I was just thinking that maybe you'd like to go to the . . . uh . . ." Man, did I have to pee. "You know . . . movies . . . tomorrow night?"

"What, me and you and Jackey?"

"Not really . . . uh . . . unless you want it that way. If you do, that's . . . uh . . . okay, I mean . . . umm . . ."

"Just me and you?"

"Yeah . . . umm . . . I mean if that's okay, but if it's not, I mean . . ."

"Like a date?"

"Uh . . ." I was up against the wall. "Yeah."

She smiled. She didn't say anything.

Great, I blew it. I made an idiot out of myself and now she's going to laugh. She must think I'm the biggest—

"Sure."

"Huh?"

"Sure, I'd like that. I've been waiting for you to ask me out."

"You have?"

"Yeah." She smiled again. She was *so* pretty.

"Uh . . . the thing is, I don't know how we'd . . . uh . . ."

"Get there?"

"Yeah."

"I'll ask Dad to drop us off. The movie starts at seven. Maybe we could eat supper at the Dairy Queen. Is that all right?"

"Uh . . . sure, I mean, if you want to, I mean . . ."

"Good. Why don't you come over around six?"

"Uh . . ."

"'Bye."

"Umm . . ." She went into the house.

The initial rush of it all knocked the wind out of me. I couldn't stand up. While I waited for my lungs to kick in, I thought about what had happened.

Am I smooth, or what? And no experience. Some of us are just born with it, I guess.

Kelly stuck her head out the door. "I figured you'd be asking me pretty soon."

"Why?"

"You've never stood outside of the living room watching me before."

Oh God, not her, too. Say so long to *my* ego.

"'Bye," she said.

"'Bye." She closed the door.

I felt stupid and ecstatic at the same time. I might have acted like a goof, but I had a date tomorrow night.

I set off through First Woods for home. The moon

came out again. Shadows jumped out of where there had been no shadows before. Something moved. It wasn't little, like a bird or a squirrel, it was big, like a man, or a monster. And then the moving thing made a little howling noise. All my good thoughts about Kelly curled up like a dry leaf in a bonfire. All of a sudden I was scared.

Now no one believes in monsters, but when you find one prowling through the woods at night, it makes you wonder. I saw this horror movie once. A werewolf stalked the woods when the moon was full, ripping people's throats out. He attacked one guy and the guy covered his throat with both hands. Instead of ripping out his throat, the werewolf ripped out something else.

Both my hands went down to cover my crotch. I didn't want nothing ripped out of nowhere. I had a date tomorrow night.

"Who is that?" I called.

The moving thing looked at me. It was all hunched over. I couldn't tell what it was.

"If you're a werewolf, I'm warning you. I have a gun with silver bullets." So what if it wasn't the truth? What would you do?

"Gyaah," the werewolf said. It stood up.

"Muddle-Head!" I never thought I'd be glad to see him, but I was. "You scared the life out of me." Almost, anyway.

"Gyaah," Muddle-Head said again. He grinned.

"What are you doing out here?" He just kept grinning. "I bet you're looking for something to steal, aren't you? Where's my teddy bear?"

He took the bear out of his bib. I strode toward him and grabbed it out of his hands. He looked at me like I'd just skewered his grandmother.

"It's mine," I said. "You stole it."

"Naah?"

"I don't care. It's mine."

That started him crying, and when Muddle-Head cried, he did his best to make sure the whole world knew it. But I didn't give in. People giving in is what got him so messed up in the first place.

I headed for the house. I could hear him bellowing all the way to the driveway. The teddy bear was so soaked with drool, I had to hold it by the ear. I didn't dare bring it in the house. I tossed it in the garage as I went by.

A strange car was parked in the driveway, a nice car with black upholstery and really shiny chrome. When I went in the kitchen, Dad was at the table, drinking beer with a big man in a suit coat with a body of muscle just beginning to turn to fat. The big man studied me but didn't say anything.

"Where have you been, Tom?" Dad asked.

"I went over to see Kelly. I asked her to the movies."

Dad smiled. "You did?"

"Yeah." I tried to keep from looking at the stranger, but he had the kind of eyes that you can't help but stare into. They freeze you where you stand, like the eyes of a snake.

"Good for you," Dad said. "What did she say?"

"She said yes. Ello is driving us in tomorrow night."

The stranger grunted, then wiped his hand over his chin. "We have business," he said. "This can wait."

Dad nodded. "Right. I'll talk to you later, son."

"What's going on?" I asked.

"He'll talk to you later," the stranger said. "Run along."

I did what he said. He looked like the kind of guy who was used to people obeying his orders.

I went out on the porch. A breeze blew through the screen, cool on my face. It made the tree branches sway, dark fingers against the lighter darkness of the sky. The stars danced between the leaves. I got so caught up in it all, I didn't notice that the stranger was leaving until I heard his car door slam. I looked up. Dad stood next to me, staring at the driveway.

"Who was that?" I asked.

"A banker. We were discussing a loan."

"Oh."

Dad sat down. We watched the banker's taillights disappear down the road.

"Where's Mom?" I asked.

"Up in her room." He smiled at me. "So you're going out with Kelly tomorrow night, huh?"

"If it's all right."

"Oh course it's all right." He leaned over next to me. "But I wouldn't tell your mother about it," he whispered. "She's been kind of . . . religious lately. You know how she is about movies. We don't want any disturbances."

"What disturbances? It's not like I'm dating the devil."

"Yeah, I know that." He looked over his shoulder into the living room, up at the ceiling, as if he could see through it to Mom in the prayer closet. "Just don't, okay?"

"Okay."

He stood and leaned on the porch railing. He breathed in deeply, smelling the night, then walked back to his chair and sat down. He stared at his hands. His eyes hung down and his mouth hung down and his skin was as loose as a bulldog's. The corners of his mouth twitched up every few seconds as if his lips wanted to say something that his mind wouldn't let them say. He stood up again.

"Good night, son."

"Good night, Dad." The bedroom door opened

and closed. I watched the night for a few minutes more, then went upstairs.

Jackey was awake. His eyes glinted in the darkness like two little fireflies.

"Who was here?" he asked.

"A banker."

"What did he want?"

"To talk about banking stuff." I crawled under the covers. "I'm taking Kelly to the movies tomorrow."

"Can I come?"

"No. It's just me and her. It's a date."

"You're taking Kelly on a date? Why?"

What a stupid question. What a stupid kid. "'Don't be a dummy."

"You gonna kiss her?"

"Think I should?"

"Kiss a darn girl? Yuck. It'd be like somebody spitting in your mouth. What if she sticks her tongue down your throat? You'd choke."

"No I wouldn't."

"How do you know?"

"I just know, that's all." Jackey is so inexperienced.

"If she has germs in her mouth, you'll get sick and die."

"If she has germs, she'd already be dead." Unless, of course, she'd developed a tolerance to them . . .

No way, couldn't be.

That's the problem with ignorants. If you're not careful when you get into a conversation with them, they'll suck your brain down until what they say starts to make sense.

"Good night, Tom."

"Good night, Jackey." His breath steadied out. The sound of it mixed with the wind through the branches.

I don't know when I fell asleep. I don't know if I did. I had too much on my mind.

CHAPTER FIFTEEN

I helped Ello fix his fence the next afternoon. Kelly helped, too. When she asked me for a nail, I jumped forty feet straight up into the air and smashed my thumb with the hammer. I tell you what, I was nervous.

I couldn't take being around her anymore, so I spent the rest of the afternoon pacing in my bedroom. When Mom asked me what was wrong, all I told her was that my thumb hurt. It wasn't a lie, not really. God would have to be a real jerk to hold it against me.

I started getting ready a little after four o'clock. I took a shower and combed my hair and flexed for a while in front of the mirror. I wanted to be pumped up when I went over to the Tohreys'. I have this awesome body, considering I don't have any muscles yet.

I checked my face for stubble. This guy at school

once told me that dating starts your hormones pumping. He'd heard of guys who before their first date had grown full beards overnight. It sounded like baloney to me, but I wasn't about to take any chances. My face was baby-butt smooth, but I lathered up and shaved anyway. I'd practiced with a razor before, and a man stuck headfirst into a barrel of starving rats couldn't have been nicked up worse. This time I didn't take any chances. I used Dad's electric.

After I finished, I splashed a little after-shave on and went to the bedroom. Jackey was lying on his bed, reading a comic book.

"You stink," he said.

"It's just after-shave. Do I really smell that bad?"

He crinkled his nose. "You must have grabbed the bug killer by mistake."

That did it. I went back in the bathroom and scrubbed my face for fifteen minutes.

When I got back, I opened the closet. "What do you think I should wear?"

"What difference does it make?"

"I want to look nice."

"Why? Kelly's seen you after you've cleaned out the pig stall. After she's seen you wearing manure, what difference does it make how you look now?"

He had a point. I ended up wearing jeans and a T-shirt, but they were my best jeans and my best T-shirt.

I was ready by five. At supper I picked at my food, saving room for the Dairy Queen.

"Are you all right?" Mom asked.

"I'm fine."

"You're not eating."

"I'm not hungry." Actually, I was starving.

"I hope you're not sick." She sighed. "Maybe you should stay in tonight."

"Mom—"

"No. It's settled. You go up to your room right after supper."

Great, just great. It had taken me six months to ask Kelly out, and now I couldn't go. By the time I'd get up the nerve to ask her again, it'd be the middle of the winter.

Dad cleared his throat. "Tom, didn't you promise to help Ello finish mending his fence tonight?" He winked at me.

"Oh . . . yeah, I almost forgot."

"No," Mom said. "If he's sick, he stays indoors."

"But Mom," Jackey said, "if he stays indoors, he won't be able to go to—" I kicked him under the table. When he looked at me, I glared. He went back to eating. He knew enough to shut up.

"It's just a little chest cold, isn't it?" Dad cupped his hands around his lips and mouthed the word "cough" to me. I did.

"You're right, Abby," he said, "he does have a

cold. He'll have to come home as soon as he's finished with the fence."

Mom sighed. "Well, all right, as long as he comes inside if the night turns chilly." She started eating again.

I tell you what, at times that Dad of mine was a pretty smart guy.

It only took me fifteen minutes to eat, or not eat, I should say. I went upstairs and sweated for fifteen more. By the time I left the house, I needed another shower.

Dad was standing on the porch when I went by. "Have fun," he said. "Don't do anything I wouldn't do."

Coming from Dad, that didn't mean much. I remember Mom giggling in the bedroom. Some joke.

I hadn't even gotten to First Woods before Jackey came running up behind me. He acted like he thought he was going somewhere.

"What do you want?"

"I'm riding in with you."

"No you're not. This is just me and Kelly. You—"

"I'm not going to the movie, just along for the ride. Mr. Tohrey said I could."

"Oh." In a way, that was all right. Having him along would give me another person to talk to if I couldn't think of what to say to Kelly.

I stood on the Tohreys' front porch with my heart

pounding in my ears. I couldn't get my arm to raise my hand to the door.

"What's the matter with you?" Jackey asked. "Aren't you gonna knock?"

"Give me a second, will you?" I bet I sweated a quart just standing there. I had to pee.

All of a sudden Jackey started digging at his crotch. He got this look on his face like the look a dog gets when you scratch behind its ears.

"Don't do that," I said.

"Do what?" He did it again.

"That. Don't scratch yourself like that. You'll embarrass me."

"How will I embarrass you? If I embarrass anyone, won't I embarrass me? I don't get embarrassed."

Some people have no manners at all. I had to threaten to blow a booger down the back of his shirt if he didn't stop. Finally he did. I forced my hand up to the door. I still wasn't ready to knock, but my knuckles shook so badly, they knocked all by themselves.

Lois answered the door. If Ello was a bear, Lois was a swan. She was tall and long and graceful. She looked like a dancer. "My, you look handsome."

"Thanks."

Jackey grunted. Lois smiled and called to Kelly. When she came to the door, she was wearing shorts and her Donald Duck T-shirt. She was *so* pretty. She had new tennies on, not the old pair stained with manure that I was used to seeing. She'd really dressed up.

"Hey, Jackey. Hey, Tom." She smiled.

"He . . . he . . . he . . ." I stopped, took a deep breath, and tried again. "He . . . he . . . he . . ."

"Hey, Kelly," Jackey said.

"You look nice, Tom."

"Thanks." It was rough going at first, but I managed to slip back into my normal cool.

Jackey snorted. "He looks like a dork. Just wait until you get in the theater. He stinks so bad from Dad's after-shave, you'll have to walk out and leave him there."

So much for cool. The butterflies banged around in my stomach so hard, I forgot to belt him. As I stood like a dummy, Ello came to the door.

"Hiya, Doc." He punched my arm.

"Hey." My voice broke. Jeez, I felt stupid.

"Everybody ready?"

"Yep," Jackey said. I didn't know if I was or not.

"Then let's go." We headed for the car.

Ello and Jackey sat in the front. Me and Kelly climbed in behind them. Jackey turned around and watched us the whole way into Elder Falls.

"Are you gonna sit in the back?" he asked.

"What?"

"At the theater. Are you gonna sit in the back?"

"You know where we sit," Kelly said. "We always sit in the middle."

"But you're on a date now," Jackey said. "Me and my friend Jason went to a movie once and sat in the back. You wouldn't believe some of the things people on dates do back there."

"Shut up, Jackey," I said.

"Sit down, Doc," said Ello.

"They're all over each other," Jackey continued. "They kiss with their mouths wide open and their hands go every which way. You wouldn't believe what I saw this one guy do. His girlfriend was wearing a skirt, and he turned in his seat and put his hand on her knee and—"

"Sit down, Doc," Ello said.

"So where are you gonna sit, Kelly?" Jackey asked.

"I don't know." She looked at me. "Where do you want to sit?"

"We can sit in the back if you like."

"The middle," Ello said. "You'll sit in the middle."

"Maybe," Jackey offered, "Kelly should have worn a skirt."

Ello dropped us off in front of the Dairy Queen, and we went in for brazier burgers and ice cream. I usually have two burgers, but I only had one that night. I didn't want to look like a pig, even though I'd eaten at the Tohreys' a ba-zillion times and Kelly knew I was a pig already. I was still starving when we walked to the Shangri-La.

The Shangri-La Theater's on Main Street, between St. Francis' Clothes for Men and Herbie's Shoe Repair. It's one of those old-style theaters with a stage and curtain. It must have a thousand seats, at least twice as many as the Elder Falls population. They built it right after the Civil War, during the Laurel and Hardy days, when they still thought Elder Falls might one day be something.

We were going to see a horror movie called *Three Nights at the Gallows*. Horror movies are the only movies I'll spend money on. The only measure of artistic excellence, I think, is how many buckets of blood you get per dollar.

I paid for our tickets, then bought a box of jujubes and a tub of popcorn the size of a garbage can. We headed into the theater.

"Where do you want to sit?" I asked.

"We better sit in the middle."

"Okay." I didn't know if I was disappointed or relieved.

So we sat in the middle row, in the middle two seats. The littler kids began gathering in the front by the stage, jumping around like a pack of wild dogs smelling blood. We didn't talk about anything. I don't know why. Every other time we went to the movies, we always had some topic to jabber about, but this time everything I thought of to say just seemed stupid. So all I did was sit there and eat popcorn. I felt like an idiot.

Robin Shaleman and her boyfriend sat in front of us. Robin was in the same class as me and Kelly, but she was older—I mean, she acted older and looked older. Boy, did she look older. All the other girls in class were still in training bras, but not Robin. She had a big one, like a 99X cup or something. If you tied her bra to a tree branch, you'd have a double swing.

"Hi, Kelly," Robin said. "Hi, Tom."

"Hey."

"This is Chuck."

"What's up, Chuck?" As soon as I said it, I felt stupid. Chuck half smiled and half glared. He'd probably heard the upchuck joke a million times. He put one arm around Robin's shoulders and rested his other hand on her knee. Robin was wearing a skirt.

I looked at Kelly. She looked at me. I grabbed a big handful of popcorn and stared at the empty screen.

After what seemed like forever, the previews started. I never paid attention to the previews. The Shangri-La's curtain never went back all the way on its own, and watching the usher try to force it was a lot more interesting. Sometimes the usher spent half the movie up there, like an extra leading man with a red jacket and lines made up of four-letter words.

This time the curtain only got halfway. The usher, a short guy with thick glasses named Sherman, ran up the aisle. As soon as he stepped on the stage, all the kids in the front pelted him with empty popcorn boxes. He stopped and cursed them, his glasses flashing in the projector's light, until the rest of the audience started cursing him, and then he turned and worked at the curtain. When it didn't come, he cursed it, too.

The screen went black after the previews. Low, weird organ music, the kind of music that vibrates your bones, rolled through the theater. Both me and Kelly scrunched in our seats. A black castle faded in on the screen. One of its spires rippled like a reflection in water as Sherman tugged on the curtain.

The castle disappeared. A warlock replaced it. His eyes were livid green and his skin the color of a corpse's lips. He leaned over a bubbling cauldron filled with a concoction that looked like the school cafeteria's soup.

"E pluribus unum," he muttered, or something like that. I didn't understand what he meant.

"YOU PIECE OF CRAP!" Sherman shouted at the curtain. That I understood.

The scene cut to the inside of a cottage, where an innocent villager sat at a table eating bread. The organ music grew louder and the warlock's chanting echoed, and all of a sudden the villager's head exploded. Blood spattered on the camera lens. The warlock's laughter echoed all around us.

"Aargh! I can't stand this!" Kelly covered her face. I popped jujubes like courage pills. This was going to be a great movie.

"Oh, Robin!" Chuck moaned.

"Oh, Chuck!" Robin moaned back.

I tell you what, those two didn't waste any time. Chuck was more in Robin's seat than he was in his own. His hand that had been on her knee scooted up her thigh. Their mouths locked together like they were trying to taste what each other had had for breakfast four days ago.

"Oh, Chuck, not here, not now!"

"I want you, Robin, I want you!"

I looked at Kelly. She was peeking through her fingers, half watching the movie, half watching Chuck and Robin, and half watching me.

I was so confused. I didn't know when I should make my move, and I didn't know what I was supposed to do when I *did* make my move. Should I do what Chuck was doing? How? Kelly wasn't wearing a skirt.

Instead of doing what I should have been doing, I watched the movie. It turned out the villager with the blown-up head lived in a German hamlet. The warlock had kidnaped the burgomaster's daughter, who also just happened to be the hero's girlfriend and the best-looking actress in the movie. The burgomaster was standing in the town square, trying to talk the villagers into storming the warlock's castle.

"Men," the burgomaster said, "an evil lurks among us, an evil that has kidnaped my beautiful daughter." The villagers generally agreed.

"It is an evil that must be eliminated." They agreed with that, too. Some even cheered.

"It is an evil only we can eliminate. We must go up to the castle! We must rout the evil out with fire!" Nobody said anything. They didn't seem too thrilled with that idea.

"YOU STUBBORN, OVERGROWN PIECE OF TOILET PAPER!" I wondered which villager was so upset. It turned out to be Sherman.

The burgomaster flustered around for a moment, then his face lit up as if he'd thought of the greatest idea since Edison invented television. "And an equal share of the castle's riches for every participating villager!"

Well, that got them going. They stormed up the castle path, shaking pitchforks and torches above their heads and trying to shout courage into each other. The only one who stayed behind was the hero.

Those villagers were just about the dumbest people I'd ever seen. You don't go chasing after a man who can pop heads like pimples on the pope's butt, I don't care how big a share you're offered. It doesn't take a genius to figure out what happened next.

The closer they got to the castle, the louder the bone-shaker music got, and right before they reached the door, the warlock's voice echoed through the theater and heads started going off like firecrackers on the Fourth of July. You've never seen so much gore. The few villagers left alive tried to run away, but they kept slipping in the splattered brains, and one by one all their heads exploded, too.

Except for the burgomaster. The warlock had something special planned for him.

The music changed, and the warlock chanted something different. All of a sudden, the burgomaster shrieked and ran toward the camera with his hands over his face. He tripped on the stump of the blacksmith's neck and skidded through the brains like a baseball player diving for home plate. When he stopped, he was only three inches from the camera. He uncovered his face.

Maggots crawled out of his eyes, out of his mouth, out of his ears, out of everywhere. They shot from his nose like boogers after a hard sneeze. He lay in the muck, screaming, until the maggots ate through his skull; then he collapsed facedown into the gore. The warlock's laughter echoed like thunder. I thought I knew what gross was. I was wrong.

"Oh, Chuck!"

"Oh, Robin!"

Jesus Criminey, how in the world could they keep their minds on making out during *that*?

The rest of the movie was calmer. The hero went on a long trek to get a magic rope to hang the warlock with. A beautiful, terrible queen owned it, but she wouldn't give it up unless he married her. They started kissing.

"Oh, Robin!"

"Oh, Chuck!"

I watched Kelly in the darkness, sweating over when the right time to kiss her would be. Shoot, the right time to kiss her was half an hour ago. I should have been lying on top of her by now. And she knew it, too. I could tell by the way she looked at me.

"Are you all right?" she asked. Her eyes said, "You dumb, inexperienced clod."

"I'm fine." But I wasn't.

"You look sick."

"I'm all right." I was starting to wish Mom had made me stay home.

I thought that maybe instead of kissing her, I'd try holding her hand, but the only time I'd ever held Kelly's hand was when we Roman wrist wrestled. She always beat me. I could see myself kneeling between the seats with my wrists bent back to the breaking point, begging for mercy. Everyone would laugh. No thanks.

I ended up just watching her watch the movie.

She'd look at me every now and then, and I could tell she wanted me to do something, but I didn't know what to do. I tried picking up pointers from Chuck, but those two were practically making babies. I don't know why they bothered to come to the movie—they weren't watching it. They could have done the same thing in Chuck's car and saved eight bucks.

The lights came on before I knew it. Everyone filed up the aisles to the exits. Sherman sat on the stage with his legs dangling over the edge, defeated. The curtain still covered a quarter of the screen.

"'Bye, Kelly. 'Bye, Tom." Robin straightened her hair. She straightened her skirt. She straightened her 99X-cup bra.

"'Bye, Robin." Kelly didn't straighten anything. I felt so stupid. I'd never had a worse time at a movie in my entire life.

Ello picked us up at the Dairy Queen. Jackey was in the front seat. He watched us all the way home.

"Did you sit in the back?" he asked.

"No."

"When you kissed her, did you have your mouth open? Did you put your hands on her knees or on her butt?"

I was too embarrassed to say anything. No, Jackey, I didn't put my hands on her butt. No, my mouth wasn't open. No, I didn't even *kiss* her. I'm just a goof that Kelly will never want to be seen with again. I don't blame her.

Jackey tried to hang around when we got back to the Tohreys', but after I threatened to beat him up, he left. Me and Kelly sat on the porch steps. My stomach was so twisted up, I thought I was going to die.

"It's pretty out tonight," she said.

"Yeah." She was *so* pretty.

"All the stars are out."

"Yeah." Jeez, I sounded like a moron. My teacher once told me I was addicted to monosyllabic grunts. I'm not sure what that means, but I know it isn't good. She said the same thing about cavemen.

"Well, I better go in."

"Okay." I leaned toward her, then leaned away again as my stomach heaved to the other side.

"I had a good time." Kelly stood up.

"Me, too." Another lie on the pile. The truth was I'd never been more miserable.

"We'll have to do it again."

"Yeah." She was just being nice.

"Good night."

"Good night." I wanted to apologize for being such a dork, but I knew if I tried, I wouldn't even get that right. I sat and suffered.

That's when she kissed me. Then she ran into the house.

I sat for a long time without moving, afraid it would all go away.

Man oh man oh man oh man. Kelly had kissed me. On the lips.

I whistled all the way through First Woods. I don't think I've ever had a better time at a movie.

CHAPTER SIXTEEN

I quit whistling as soon as I hit the pasture. A sheriff's-department car was in the driveway, its lights flashing. I ran the rest of the way home.

Dad stood on the lawn with a deputy. Mom was on the porch with her hand on Jackey's shoulder, watching them through the screen door.

"Are you sure that's all that was taken?" the deputy asked. "Just your television?"

"That's it," Dad answered.

Jesus Criminey. Someone had robbed us.

"Where was everyone when this happened?"

"The boys were at the Tohreys'. Abby was upstairs."

"Where were you?"

"Outside."

"And you didn't see anything?"

"I was down by the creek."

"What about you, Abby?" the deputy asked.

Mom sniffled once. "I heard something, someone bustling around downstairs."

"And you didn't do anything?"

"I thought it was John." Her breath caught in her throat. "Dear Lord Jesus, protect us. There was a stranger in our house! He could have come upstairs, he could have . . ." One hand clutched her breast as she leaned against the door frame.

"Take it easy," the deputy said.

Dad stepped onto the porch and took Mom's arm. "Why don't you have a seat in the living room, Abby? I don't think you're needed out here anymore." He looked over his shoulder. "Is she?"

"No." Dad led Mom indoors, then came back outside.

The deputy scribbled something in his notebook. "We'll see what we can do."

"I hope you catch whoever's responsible," Dad said.

"I do, too. Good night, Jack."

"Good night, Harv." The deputy walked past me to the car. We watched him drive to the road. Dad led me and Jackey into the living room.

Mom huddled on the couch. Her face quivered in a thousand directions at once. Tears trembled down her cheeks and her voice shook. "What's going to happen to us?"

174

"Nothing's going to happen to us," Dad said.

All of a sudden Jackey ran back to the door. "My chickens! Did anybody check my chickens?"

"Why?"

"What if they were stolen?"

I shook my head. "Nobody's going to steal your chickens."

"What if Chester's stolen?"

"Least of all, nobody's going to steal Chester."

"You don't know that. Chester's a special chicken. Chester!" He ran out the door. I didn't try to stop him. I was a kid once, and I used to do stupid things, too.

Mom closed her eyes. She leaned forward until her head rested on her knees.

"Oh most merciful Father, in these times of trial and tribulation . . ."

A prayer was the last thing I needed to hear. I went up to my room.

I was already under the covers when Jackey came up. He put on his pajamas, hopped on his bed, and picked up a comic book.

"Chester's all right," he said, as if I'd asked. "Nobody stole her."

"I told you. Nobody'd want to steal a runt like that."

Jackey glared at me. "Don't say that."

"Runt!"

"I said don't say that!"

"Runt, runt, runt, runt, runt."

Jackey picked up his piggy bank and threw it at me. I caught it just before it smashed into the wall.

"Don't make noise! All's we need is Mom up here."

"Then take that back!"

"I'm not taking anything back about a runt chicken."

Jackey picked up the clock. "Take it back or I throw this on the floor."

"Jackey—"

"I mean it!"

"All right, I take it back." He set the clock down.

Kids. You can't live with them. I'd sure like to try to live without them.

While Jackey read his comic book, I tried to think about the burglary. I couldn't. Every thought I had kept drifting back to Kelly and our date. Jeez, it had been something. It was the best time I'd ever had.

Someday, I'll take Kelly on dates everywhere. We'll see that big red square they got in Moscow, and we'll spray paint graffiti on the Great Wall of China, and we'll drop bowling balls off the Leaning Tower of Pisa, just like Galileo did. We'll go everywhere and we'll do everything, and she'll be smooching me the whole time. I tell you what, I can't wait.

Jackey fell asleep, the comic book over his face. I

got up, set it on his nightstand, and turned off the light. As I climbed into bed, I happened to look out the window. Lucky I did.

Someone was crawling through the shadows. I watched for a minute. It was Muddle-Head.

Well, that sure explained a lot.

Mom said that someone had broken into the house. It wasn't a someone at all—it was Muddle-Head. Old Muddle-Head had gone beyond stealing teddy bears. Now he was up to TV's. I bet he could sell a TV like ours for almost fifty dollars. He was just playing stupid so no one would suspect him. Muddle-Head was a lot smarter than he let himself on to be.

I thought about running down and telling Mom and Dad I knew who the burglar was, but I decided against it. They were always siding with the big dope—they'd never believe me. If I got slapped for calling him Muddle-Head, what would happen if I called him a burglar?

No, I decided, the best way to handle it was to watch and wait and listen. If Muddle-Head stole once, he'd steal again, and when he did, whammo! I'd nail him.

Play it cool, I thought. Playing it cool has always been my specialty.

CHAPTER SEVENTEEN

The last class of the day during the fall quarter was English. We were studying Abraham Lincoln's speeches. He wrote "Four score and seven years ago." What's the matter with writing "Eighty-seven"? That's just what I mean about writers. He and Mark Twain must have sat around together talking about how to write goofy. While Abe was running for president, a girl told him to grow a beard, so he did. What a dummy. I suppose if she'd told him to jump off a cliff, he'd have done that, too.

Is it just coincidence that the only president who listened to girls was also the only president to have civil war during his administration? I don't think so.

The only thing anyone could talk about on the bus ride home was the burglaries. We'd been robbed a month earlier, and they were still going on.

"Who do you think is doing it?" Kelly asked. She sat next to me on the bus. She always did now. We had this boyfriend/girlfriend thing going. We'd smooched I bet a hundred times since that first movie. I was getting pretty good at it. Of course, I was pretty good when I started.

"I bet it's somebody from the Twin Cities," Jimmy Holfield said. Minneapolis and St. Paul are Minnesota's Sodom and Gomorrah. If you look back while driving out of one of them, you'll turn into a pillar of salt.

But the Cities weren't to blame this time. I knew who the burglar was—Muddle-Head. I didn't say anything, though. I couldn't yet prove it. But I would. I would have bet a ba-zillion dollars on it.

"Shoot," Jimmy said, "we lost our microwave just last weekend. We can't make microwave popcorn anymore."

"That's tough," I said.

"And George Shade lost a set of wrenches." Jackey nodded.

"Well, if the burglar ever shows up at my place," Tony Bingham said, "I'll just pop him a good one in the mouth, and that'll be the end of him." Tony always talked big, because talk was all he could do. He was about two foot four and weighed fifty pounds. When he slapped mosquitoes, they grinned at him.

"That ain't nothing," Jimmy said. "Joe Tristam

told my dad that if the burglar shows up at his place, he's gonna blast him. He's keeping a loaded shotgun by the door."

"He always keeps a loaded shotgun by the door," I said.

"He'd shoot Santa Claus," Tony said.

"He would?" Jackey's eyes got big. I don't think he still believed in Santa, but he was young enough to not risk losing Christmas presents by letting anyone know that. But who can tell what ignorants believe?

"Right between the eyes." Tony grinned.

I shook my head. "No he wouldn't. That's enough of that, Tony." I glared at him, and Tony backed down. I didn't like people teasing Jackey. If he needed teasing, then I'd do it.

"Why doesn't Joe just sic Muddle-Head on the burglar?" Jimmy asked.

"Yeah," I said, "he could drool him to death."

We all laughed, except Kelly and Jackey. Jackey didn't because he was still young enough to think of Muddle-Head as a friend. Kelly didn't because she was a girl, and girls wouldn't know good humor if it jumped up and slapped them in the face. They're just one step up from muddle-heads themselves. Monkeys, muddle-heads, girls, guys. It's evolution. Charlie Darwin wrote all about it.

When we got home, Mom was in the kitchen,

brewing coffee. "I just finished baking chocolate-chip cookies," she said.

"All right!" Chocolate-chip cookies are my favorite.

"Join your father on the porch." She handed me and Jackey each a big glass of milk, then led us out to the porch with a cup of coffee for Dad and tea for herself. She went back into the kitchen after the cookies.

Dad was relaxing in his chair. He was relaxing a lot more now than he used to. Somehow he'd gotten the money together to make the fall payment. I didn't know if he got it from a new loan or what. It probably had something to do with that banker.

"How was school?" he asked.

"Same as always," I said.

The wind through the screen was chilly—fall was setting in. The leaves were turning, as if, from somewhere deep inside them, red and orange fire was eating through the green. In fall, everything bursts into life just before it dies, from leaves to butchered chickens.

Mom stepped onto the porch with a pyramid of the best cookies in the world balanced on a plate. I made a grab, but she slapped my hand.

"We give thanks before we eat in this house," she said.

"Okay. Rub-a-dub-dub, thanks for the grub." I

made another grab and she slapped me again.

"We give *proper* thanks before we eat in this house."

Jeez, it was only cookies. It wasn't like Thanksgiving or anything.

"Bow your heads." We did. "Oh most merciful Father," she prayed, "we thank you for your bountiful blessings on us, your children. Bless this food to our bodies that we may be worthy of your service. Amen." I made another grab. This time she didn't stop me.

Jackey pried a chocolate chip loose and stuck it up his nose.

"What are you doing?" Mom asked.

He screamed and shook his head. The chip popped out. He gobbled it down.

"What," Mom repeated, "are you doing?"

"I'm being a master burger," Jackey said.

"A what?"

"A master burger. He was in a movie Tom saw. He had bugs crawling out of his nose and everything."

Mom glared at me. "What is this about a movie?"

"Uh . . ." I froze stone cold.

"You know I forbid you to see that filth."

"Leave him alone, Abby," Dad said. "If you want someone to blame, blame me. I said he could go." That's not entirely true, but if Dad wanted to bear the brunt of Mom's holy wrath, I wasn't about to stop him.

182

"You know what those movies are, John! They're enticements of the flesh!" She set her cup down, stared at it for a moment, then picked it up again. "It's hard enough for my boys to remain pure without being tempted by half-naked seducers on a screen. I won't have it!"

"What's a seducer?" Jackey asked.

"Be quiet, John, Jr.," Mom said.

"But all's I wanted to know—"

"I said be quiet!"

The wind whispered through the screen. Nobody said a word. Jackey grabbed another cookie.

"Is a seducer like the girls who wear skirts in the back of the theater?"

"What?" Mom asked.

"Because if it is, Tom, you better not sit back there anymore with Kelly."

Why, the little snitch. "Shut up, Jack—"

Mom cut me off. She looked at Jackey. "Tom was sitting where with Kelly?"

"In the back of the theater. Boy oh boy, you should hear about some of the stuff they did back there. Once he put his hand under her shirt, and—"

Mom dropped her cup on the floor. The splashing tea bit my leg like hot teeth. Her hands shook, her head shook, her jaw muscles pumped in and out like a heart beating.

"I did not, Mom!" I said. And I didn't. There's a big difference between what a person says and what

183

he does. Jackey had wanted stories, so I had given him stories. Now I wished I hadn't.

Mom stared at me for a long time. Finally, she stood, pushed the screen door open, and marched toward the pasture.

"Abby?" Dad asked.

"The little whore," she said.

"Abby!"

"The little whore!" When she reached the barn, she broke into a run. Dad ran after her.

"Real good, Jackey," I said.

"What did I do?"

I followed Mom and Dad.

"What did I do?" Jackey called after me.

By the time I reached the pasture, Mom was almost to First Woods. Dad was sprinting past the sledding hill toward her. He caught her right on the pasture's edge. I was twenty yards behind them, still running. When Mom turned and slapped Dad across the face, I stopped in my tracks.

"How could you?" she screamed. "How could you allow this?"

Dad grabbed her arms, just above the elbows. "Abby—"

"Let me go! I will not have a demon seducer like that tempt my boy out of God's keeping." She turned her head and screamed into the woods. "Come out here, you little whore!"

184

Dad still held her elbows. She scratched his forehead hard enough to draw blood. When he didn't let go, she kicked his shin.

"Abby!" He shook her, hard. She scratched him again.

"Abby! She's just a girl!"

"Demon!" Mom screamed. "Whore!"

This time Dad slapped Mom. She stared at him, shocked, her fingers curved and trembling. The ends of her nails were stained red.

"She's just a girl, Abby." Blood ran down his forehead. "She's not a demon or a whore or a seducer. She's just a girl."

Mom stared at him, her mouth half open. Her fingers relaxed as big tears began rolling down her cheeks. She collapsed to the ground. Dad went down with her, cradling her shoulders in his arm.

"My boys," she sobbed. "Everything's leaving us. Who's going to take care of my boys?"

Blood ran over the bridge of Dad's nose. "They'll be all right. You know that."

"But if God provides . . ." She tried to wipe the blood off his face but only smeared it. Dad smiled. She buried her face in his chest and sobbed. "Tell me, John. Please tell me."

"Tell you what, Abby?"

"Tell me everything will be all right. Tell me I'm going to be happy again."

185

"You're going to be happy again, Abby." He picked her up in his arms and walked back toward me. With every sob, Mom's body shook. Her hair hid Dad's eyes. His lips murmured softly next to her ear. "Everything will be just fine. You'll see."

"I can't see. I can't see anything at all. I'm so tired, John. I've never been this tired in my life."

He pulled her shoulders tight into his chest. "We have to be strong now," he said softly. "Do you understand?" She looked at him for a long time, nodded, then buried her face in his chest again. She was still crying.

Dad pointed with his chin toward the house. "Tom, why don't you get Mom's bed ready for her, the one downstairs." When I didn't move, he smiled. "Everything's fine now," he said. "Do as I say."

I ran back to the house. Dad brought Mom in, then went to call the doctor. While he was on the telephone, me and Jackey pulled the covers over her. Mom was half sleeping, half crying. She looked all used up. I guess she was.

After calling the doctor, Dad called Gramma. When he was through talking to her, he went in the bedroom, shooed us out, and closed the door. Mom was still crying when the doctor arrived, still crying when he left. Gramma came out to fix us supper. Grampa wouldn't come.

It was after our bedtime when Mom finally

quieted down. Me and Gramma and Jackey were waiting in the living room when Dad came out.

Gramma set her knitting down. "Is she all right?"

"She's sleeping."

"But is she all right?"

"She's fine."

"What did the doctor say?"

"She needs rest. She's had a breakdown."

Jackey looked up. "What's that mean?"

Dad sat in the rocking chair and rubbed his face with his hands. The dried blood flaked under his fingers.

"It means," he said, "that she's found her salvation." Jackey looked puzzled. Dad smiled.

"It means she's fine. Why don't you two go up to bed?"

CHAPTER EIGHTEEN

We butchered a week later, me and Dad and Jackey. Mom was still in bed.

It took a long time for her to get better. While we crept around the house on tippy-toes, she stayed in their bedroom and rested.

"I can't stand it anymore!" she shouted one day. "Someone make some noise!" We gladly obliged her.

As soon as she was back on her feet, she went upstairs and closed the prayer closet down. She stripped the bed and took out the lamp and sheets and put the picture of Jesus back downstairs where it belonged. She dusted it first.

Mom changed. She still made us go to church on Sundays, but we didn't have to go during the week unless we wanted to, so naturally we didn't. We still prayed before every meal, but not before cookies.

"I still don't like those movies," she told me, "but if you want to go, you can. I trust your discretion. And I trust your discretion with Kelly, too."

All in all, she was a whole lot calmer. What's the word Dad used? Serene. Mom was serene. She found out there's a lot less evil in the world than she thought there was.

Winter came. It wasn't nearly as cold as the one before had been, at least not until the very end. Just when you'd think spring would come along, it got cold and snowed five inches. It was like someone upstairs got the seasons backward.

"God," Clint always said, "is dyslexic."

One night while Mom was in town getting groceries, me and Jackey went over to the Tohreys', me to see Kelly and Jackey to goof around. Ello was working on Molly again. He wanted to show me more about how she worked, but I'd already learned as much about tractors as I cared to. I headed home. Kelly helped Ello. Jackey chased a cat.

When I got back, the banker's car was in the driveway. From the entryway, I could see Dad and the banker sitting in the kitchen. They weren't joking and they weren't laughing and they weren't drinking beer. They hunched over the table like generals discussing war plans. I wondered what they were talking about.

"Tom!" Dad said when I stepped into the kitchen.

"I thought you went over to the Tohreys'."

"I did. I came back. What's going on?"

"Are the chores done?"

"Not yet. What—"

"Why don't you go do the chores?" He smiled and rested his hand on my shoulder.

"What are you talking about? Loans again?"

The banker grunted, then half smiled. "Yeah," he said, "loans again. Go do your chores."

I went outside. When I finished feeding the animals, I crept in the house through the front door and hid in the living-room shadows. The banker was leaning back in his chair, watching Dad. Dad hunched over the table, staring at his hands. His face was gray and his fingers trembled.

"It's like this every time," the banker said.

Dad shrugged. He didn't answer.

The stranger wiped his nose between his thumb and forefinger. "Are you sure you know what to do?"

"Yeah, I'm sure."

"Good. Then do it." He stood and walked toward the entryway, then stopped. "You said you wanted to keep this place."

"I do."

"Then change your attitude. I'm tired of putting up with it. I can always find someone else. There's plenty like you."

"I know. Don't worry about me."

"Don't give me a reason to. I'll see you next week."

"Right." The banker lumbered out the back door. A moment later, his car rumbled down the driveway.

Dad came into the living room. He took a step back when he saw me. "I didn't know you were in here."

"Only for a couple of minutes. Did you get the loan?"

Dad sighed and sat down. "I don't know. We'll have to see. Why'd you come back from the Tohreys' so early?"

"Ello was working on his tractor. I didn't want to bother him."

Dad slouched in his chair. He looked as old as I'd ever seen him.

"What's the matter?" I asked.

"Nothing."

"Oh."

It sure looked like there was, but if he said there wasn't, then there wasn't. Like I said, me and Dad didn't lie to each other.

CHAPTER NINETEEN

Later on that night, while I was lying in bed listening to Jackey snore, something banged outside. I looked out the window. Muddle-Head was wandering through the yard.

"What have you come to steal this time?" I whispered.

He stood under the yard light, grinning up as if he wanted to fly to it, like a moth. He looked at the house, then at the garage. He hiked his overalls up, let them fall again, and went in the garage through the side door.

"He's after the teddy bear again," I said, and sure enough, a moment later he came out with it clutched in his hand. He held it against his cheek, petted it, then disappeared into the shadows.

I'd had as much out of him as I was going to take.

It was time to nail old Muddle-Head.

Our bedroom window was right above the porch roof, and it only took me a second to change, throw on an extra sweater, climb outside, and shinny down the apple tree growing at the corner of the house—Dad once made the mistake of telling me how he and Eugene used to sneak out at night. I slunk to the garage around the circle the yard light threw. Muddle-Head's big old clumsy feet had left tracks, and I followed them until it was too dark to see. They headed back toward the Tristam place.

Something rustled in the brush in front of me, and I froze like a prowling cat. It rustled again, and then there was the sharp sound of ice breaking. Muddle-Head was following the creek home. I slunk down to the creek's bank, then made my way upstream toward the Tristams'. Once the moon came out and I saw Muddle-Head in front of me, his arms held out from his sides and the teddy bear clutched in one hand, swaying back and forth, dancing. He looked like some kind of a loony—what am I saying, he *was* a loony. I hid in the shadows and waited until the clouds covered the moon again.

Muddle-Head never suspected me, not the whole time he followed the creek. He climbed the slope when he reached his place. I waited a few minutes, then climbed up after him. Any second now I expected him to lead me to where he'd stashed all the stuff he'd been stealing over the last several months. Any second now I expected to get our TV back. Now that Mom had her religion under control, maybe we could watch real shows again.

Someone was in the Tristam barn. The light was on, anyway. Muddle-Head's stupid smile broadened as he stood by the door. All of a sudden he quit smiling. He backed away, scared.

Joe stepped out of the barn. Joe's face was always red, like he had a perpetual sunburn, but now it was even redder than usual. There was an anger there I had never seen before—not in his face, not in anyone's. I hid farther back in the bushes.

"Where have you been, you dimwit?" Joe demanded.

"Pa." Muddle-Head raised his hands. "Gyaah!"

"When I tell you to stay home, I mean for you to stay home!" Joe slapped Muddle-Head's cheek hard enough to knock him down. Muddle-Head bellowed. Joe kicked him in the chest, hard, cutting off Muddle-Head's cry like he'd taken a cleaver to him.

"What's the matter with you?" Joe shouted.

Muddle-Head coughed. Joe kicked him again. "Answer me!"

Muddle-Head curled into a ball, his arms covering his head. "Pa!"

"You're no son of mine!" Joe strode away three steps, then came back again. He leaned over Muddle-

Head. "Do you hear me, dimwit? You're no son of mine!"

"Pa?" Muddle-Head asked. He started crying. He didn't bellow this time, only long, slow tears that reflected the light from the barn. He hugged the teddy bear to his chest.

"Get into the barn," Joe ordered.

Muddle-Head just kept crying and hugging the teddy bear.

"I said get into the barn! Why do I have to repeat everything?" Joe shook his head. "You dumb retard." He grabbed Muddle-Head by the hair and dragged him toward the barn. Muddle-Head crawled after him, one hand dragging the teddy bear through the snow, leaving a little trail. I watched until they were inside. I heard a sound like a whip cracking. Muddle-Head bellowed again.

I slipped down the slope to the creek, then followed the bank back to our place. I didn't once look up. I kept my eyes on the creek.

I used to think there were werewolves in the woods. I used to think there were monsters in the movies. But the werewolves aren't in the woods. And the monsters aren't in the movies, either.

CHAPTER TWENTY

Dad went into town the next night. Mom and me and Jackey ate an early dinner, then I went for a walk.

It was a warm night, but not above freezing. As I strolled down the road, I listened to the little silent sounds in the trees. Their buds were swelling; they were as anxious for spring as I was. The last sliver of sun disappeared behind the western fields, and the sunset shone fiery red, heat against the cold. It was so pretty it caught in my throat.

I walked by the Tohreys', away from the Tristams'. I didn't want to go by there.

I thought about asking Kelly to join me, but then I decided against it. There's something about winter walks that says you have to do them alone. During the other seasons, the woods are already noisy with birds and squirrels and other animals crashing through the brush, and a little extra noise doesn't harm anything, but winter is always silent and its beauty is silent, and having another person along, another set of footsteps and another voice, kills part of the beauty. I've always thought that, even when I was a kid.

I went past their house, past the Holfields', all the way down to where the creek cut south across the road. I followed it for maybe half a mile before I set off across the fields for home. I saw rabbit tracks in the ditch, deer poop in a corn field, and, just before I hit Little Crow's field, fox tracks jogging away through the trees. I even heard something scratching inside an old dead snag in a windbreak. It was probably a raccoon. I didn't bother him. I wouldn't want him knocking on my door, so I didn't knock on his.

I walked up one side of Little Crow's hill and down the other. Halfway up the driveway, I ran right smack into Jesus. He stopped me dead in my tracks.

I could feel Him all around me, everywhere. It wasn't a bad feeling, the way it was in church or in the prayer closet. In those places, He always wanted to send someone to Hell. Maybe what I hated was not so much Jesus as what people *said* about Jesus, and maybe what they said was all wrong. Maybe Jesus wasn't so much an angry tyrant as He was a god who just wanted to sit on your front porch and drink a beer with you. Maybe all Jesus wanted was to be your friend.

I don't know, I'm no theologian. Maybe I should have just listened to the Reverend—after all, he'd studied Jesus his whole life. Of course, Clint had, too.

"Jesus," Clint always said, "is like nobody you've ever heard about." Which was probably true.

Jackey was pulling on my sleeve. I'd been so busy pondering, I hadn't noticed him.

"Come quick," he said. "Cleo just about killed Chester." He sprinted for the shed.

I sighed. Here we go again.

Chester crouched under the corner, and she looked bad. She must have been hiding there when Cleo strutted by, and Cleo must have pecked her hard enough to draw blood. Chickens go crazy when they smell blood.

"I don't know, Jackey. I don't know about this at all." Cleo had pecked her eyes out. Her throat was open and red with blood. At first I thought she was dead, but when I reached down to touch her, she scuttled farther under the shed.

"Will she be okay?"

"I don't think so." Any fool could see she was dying.

"Maybe we could take her to the doctor."

"Maybe. He might be able to fix her neck, but she doesn't have eyes anymore." I put my hand on his shoulder. "She's blind. That's no way to live."

"Maybe he could give her new eyes."

"No Jackey, only God can do that, and then only by a miracle. God won't waste a miracle on just a chicken."

Tears came to his eyes. "Chester's not just a chicken. Chester's *my* chicken. She's been my friend for two years."

"I can't help that, Jackey. He won't do it."

"Maybe if we pray real hard. I'll get Mom to pray real hard." He ran toward the house. I stood in the cold and waited. Poor kid.

Mom said she'd pray. We sat together, wrapped in blankets, in the empty brooder house. Chester lay in a box on Jackey's knees, covered by a scrap of cloth. She was so weak she couldn't raise her head.

So we sat, and Mom prayed and Jackey prayed and I waited for Chester to die.

The whole world was quiet. The full moon shone through the window, right on Chester's box. When I looked down, I saw that she wasn't breathing. I didn't say anything, because I figured maybe she'd start up again. She didn't.

"She's dead, Jackey."

"She's resting."

"She quit breathing."

Jackey took his mitten off and gently touched her chest. He left his hand there for a moment, then drew it back and slowly put his mitten on. He started to cry. Big, silent tears dripped from his cheeks to dot the blanket. Mom put her arm around his shoulders.

"Why'd Cleo do it? What did Chester ever do to her?"

"It's just the way things are," I said. "It's the pecking order." That was an awfully stupid reason.

"But Cleo killed her. Cleo didn't have to kill her, did she? She didn't have to . . ." He was crying too hard to finish.

"It's all right, John, Jr." Mom held his head to her chest and rocked him like a baby. "To everything there is a season, a time to be born and a time to die. Tonight was Chester's time."

"It isn't fair. Cleo killed her. All Chester wanted was a fair chance, and Cleo killed her. Why?"

Mom whispered something in his ear. He laid his head in her lap, still holding the box, and cried.

"I don't want to take care of the chickens no more," he said.

"You don't have to," I told him. "I'll do it."

Mom stroked his hair back off his forehead and let him cry. I figured it would be best if I left them alone. I went outside.

A few minutes later, Mom and Jackey came out, too. Jackey held the box in his hands. He wasn't crying anymore. He didn't look up or say anything.

"We're going to have a funeral," Mom said.

"All right."

"We're going to bury Chester in First Woods. Jackey and I will start out now. You get a shovel and follow us."

"All right." I watched them go. Jackey looked so lonely carrying that box, I thought I was going to cry.

I went to the utility shed for a shovel, then started for First Woods. As I walked by the coop, I stopped. I leaned the shovel against the wall and went inside.

Cleo was sitting on her nest, cleaning her feathers. When she saw me, she clucked and stretched out her neck.

"You're immortal, aren't you, Cleo?" I asked her. "Nothing can touch you."

She clucked again. I scratched her. She made me so mad I wanted to scream.

As I scratched, she settled deeper in her nest like the queen of the world working her big butt into her throne. My fingers closed around her throat and I yanked her up into the air. I thought about giving her a quick snap, but I wanted her to know what was coming, and I wanted the other

201

chickens to see it. When she realized what was happening, she squawked and flapped, but it didn't do her any good.

I looked her in the eye, her little, frightened, blood-red eye. "You're never big enough, Cleo," I told her. "There's always someone bigger than you are."

Her beak cracked open in a half gasp; then I rung her around quick twice. The bones in her neck snapped like a whisper and then she was dead. The other hens scuttled around my feet, frightened out of their wits. Cleo hung limp from my hand.

"There's always someone bigger than you are," I repeated for the rest of them. I went outside. I tossed Cleo's body behind the barn before heading for First Woods.

Mom and Jackey were waiting for me beneath an oak tree. The ground was too hard to dig in, so I made a hole in the snow and Jackey put Chester in it. I knew a fox or dog would get her, but I didn't say anything about that. Maybe they'd get Cleo first.

"Lord," Mom prayed, "we commit to you the body and soul of Chester. Bless her and guide her into your keeping." She sprinkled a handful of snow on the box.

Jackey made a cross out of two sticks and stuck it in the bank by her head. He was crying too hard to say anything. He sprinkled his snow, then buried his face in Mom's coat.

"Good-bye, Chester," I said softly. "You were a good chicken. The best of them."

I shoveled snow over the grave, stood by respectfully for a moment, then left Mom and Jackey to mourn. I've never been one for funerals.

CHAPTER TWENTY-ONE

The next night, Dad was in town again, doing something. Me and Kelly played Kill the Turd. Jackey didn't play. He was still in mourning.

I was the turd, and when Kelly slid down the hill she almost annihilated me. I didn't mind. I liked getting annihilated by Kelly.

She was lying on top of me, crosswise, with a knee jammed in one ear and an elbow in the other.

"Are we ever going to outgrow this?" she asked.

"I hope not," I said. She laughed and pecked me on the cheek, then climbed back up the hill.

We were gathering the mini boggans together after a really good collision when a gunshot echoed in the air, rolling like a May thunderstorm. It came from Joe Tristam's place.

"What do you suppose he shot now?" I asked. I hoped it wasn't Merle.

"With Joe, who knows?"

I picked up my mini boggan. "Maybe a skunk."

Kelly started up the hill. "I bet it's another mail-man." We both laughed.

We sledded for maybe another hour, and then a sheriff's car pulled up in our driveway, its lights flashing. We looked at each other, then without saying anything ran for the house.

A deputy, the same one who had come out the night the TV was stolen, stood by the car. He stopped us before we went inside.

"What's going on?" I asked.

He didn't say anything at first. "I'll let your mother tell you." He looked us over. "Do you both live here?"

Kelly shook her head. "I live at the Tohrey place."

"Why don't you run along home?"

"But we were in the middle of—"

"You can finish whatever you were doing later. Run along home."

Kelly didn't argue. She squeezed my hand, then set off across the pasture.

I must have been waiting with the deputy for a ba-zillion hours before the sheriff came out. He looked at me, then at the deputy.

"Is this the other one?" he asked.

"Yeah."

The sheriff nodded. "You can go inside now," he told me.

"What happened?"

"Your mom will tell you. Let's get out of here, Harv." They got in the car and drove away.

I stripped my coat and snow pants off in the entryway. Mom was sitting on the living-room sofa, her hands clasped loosely in her lap. She stared at them without any expression on her face at all.

"What happened, Mom?"

"Your brother's upstairs. Call him down."

"But—"

"Call your brother." I did as she said.

When Jackey came down, we stood in front of her. She still didn't look up.

"What happened, Mom?"

She sighed. It was a long time before she spoke. "There was an accident."

A hollow feeling crawled into my stomach. "What kind of an accident?"

"Your father . . ." Her voice caught.

"Mom," Jackey asked, "where's Dad?"

"Your father . . ." She began to cry. She reached for Jackey, pulled him into her lap, and wept into his hair. She reached for me, too, but I didn't go. Instead, I went outside. I forgot to put on my coat.

The moon was bright and the north wind cold as it crept through my shirt. I followed the driveway down to the road, then crossed it and climbed Little Crow's hill. I thought about the time I'd followed

Dad out to the hill, the time I'd seen him cry.

I thought about a lot of things as I stood there. I thought about the banker and how Dad was always gone at nights. I thought about the money Dad had to pay the loans. I thought about the burglaries and the gunshot coming from Joe Tristam's.

The snow-white fields rose and fell like ocean swells in the moonlight. They stretched around me for miles, firm and solid and strong, but changing at the same time. The wind rolled up the hillside and tossed cold snow in my face. The fields were swells and the snow was foam, and I was a sailor alone at sea in the dead of the night.

I've never seen the sea, but I've seen the land, and it's just about the prettiest thing that could ever be. It doesn't surprise me that Little Crow fought to keep it, and it doesn't surprise me that Great-Great-Great-Grampa Justin did, either. The only thing that would surprise me is if they hadn't.

It's funny how you can know something and not know it at the same time. It's funny how you can convince yourself to believe a lie.

I knew what Mom was going to say. I just didn't want to hear her say it.

CHAPTER TWENTY-TWO

Dad's funeral was three days later. The family showed up, but not many neighbors, just George Shade and the Tohrey family. I couldn't sit with Kelly. Me and Mom and Jackey had to sit in the front pew by ourselves.

It was an open-casket funeral. Joe shot Dad in the back while he was running away from the house. The only thing Joe lost was the radio Dad dropped when he fell, and a shotgun slug. Now Dad lay in front of us, as if the Reverend's sermon had bored him to sleep. He'd always been quiet in church. I couldn't look at him.

The Reverend Carstairs sat behind the pulpit. He looked older somehow, and softer. His eyes were dry. He looked more like a normal person than I'd ever seen him look.

Maybe when you get old, death does that to you. Maybe death makes you human.

Mrs. Hemmer played the organ, softer than on Sundays. When she finished, the Reverend Carstairs told us all about where Dad was born, what he did as a kid, when he married Mom, and how he lived as a farmer. He didn't say much about his dying. He just said he died.

After he finished, the fat alto that sat next to Mrs. Kramer in the choir sang a song about gardens and dew on roses and joy that none other has ever known. When she finished, the Reverend stood up again.

"John Morrell," he said, "was a simple man of the earth, a man as strong and pure and honorable as the earth. John Morrell was a good man. Some may not agree with me, but John Morrell was the best man I ever knew."

The Reverend licked his lips and adjusted the microphone. He wiped his eyes with the back of his hand.

"Where," he asked, "does a good man go wrong? Is it in his character? No, for John was a man of character. Is it in his friends, or in his family? No, for John's friends were good friends, and his family a good family. Where does a good man go wrong?" He stared at the Bible lying open on the pulpit. At last he shook his head.

"I don't know," he said. "I just don't know."

He stopped. His gnarled old fingers trembled. Finally he looked up.

"May God have mercy on the soul of John William Morrell. May God have mercy on all our souls." He sat down again.

Mrs. Hemmer started playing as the ushers came forward. When I looked up, one of them motioned to me to approach the casket. I didn't want to. I didn't move. Mom put her arm around my shoulders.

I looked at her. Her long red hair—auburn she called it—glowed faintly against the blackness of her dress. Her eyes brimmed with tears, but as I watched, she smiled.

Southern Baptist Southern Belle. That's what Dad had called her.

"We have to be strong now," she whispered. "Do you understand?"

I nodded and rose. It didn't do any good. I couldn't make my feet move. Finally, she took my hand in hers, and with Jackey's in her other hand, she led us toward the casket. Mom always led us everywhere.

The body didn't look anything like Dad. It had makeup on and was soft-looking. Its hair was combed and its face was pale and there wasn't a spot of dirt or sweat anywhere. It couldn't have been my dad, be-cause my dad would have wanted to be buried looking like he just came in from a long day in the fields. This guy wasn't my dad at all.

Mom squeezed my hand. When I looked at her, a single tear ran down her cheek to settle in a crease at the corner of her mouth. She raised her hand and wiped the tear away with the back of my fingers. It felt cool and wet.

We sat back down. The rest of the mourners filed past. Some, like Gramma Morrell, looked at the casket for a long, long time. Others walked past quickly without looking at all. Grampa Morrell walked slowly up to the body, then rested his trembling palm on Dad's crossed hands.

"I'm sorry, son," he said, his voice harsh and rasping. "I didn't know. I didn't understand." He dropped his cane and collapsed to his knees and cried against the side of the casket. Two old guys I didn't know came forward and helped him to his feet. He was crying when he walked by me. So was Jackey. So was I.

After everyone had gone by, the funeral director closed the casket. The Reverend called for the pallbearers. They carried it out to the hearse. We got in a limo behind it.

Roger Kramer, in his police uniform, straddled his motorcycle and led the procession slowly through the bright sunshine toward the cemetery. All around us the snow was melting. In the yards, spots of new green grass peeked out. One old woman stood with her hands on her hips, examining a tulip bed. They'd be blooming anytime now.

The cemetery was by the lake, directly across from the city park and right next to a drive-in root beer stand. We crawled through the maze of cemetery roads until we reached a small hill. On its summit stood the mausoleum. They couldn't bury Dad until the ground thawed.

We left the cars and followed the pallbearers up the hill. When we reached the top, the Reverend stopped in front of the casket and opened his Bible. He bowed his head. Everyone else did, too.

Someone walked up behind me. I turned my head. It was Merle. He was wearing the coveralls with only one shoulder strap. The crotch hung to his knees—you'll never see Merle on the cover of GQ.

"Hi, Merle," I whispered. "I'm glad you're here."

He looked at me with those little bright eyes of his and grinned. He reached beneath the coveralls' bib and took out his teddy bear. He cuddled it to his chest.

"And now, John William Morrell," the Reverend said, "we commit your soul to the keeping of Almighty God. May He protect and guide you until His return, and your resurrection. Amen."

The Reverend closed his Bible and walked slowly to his car. Mom took Jackey's hand and followed him. Merle stood by the casket until everyone but me was gone; then he nestled the teddy bear into the flowers resting on it and walked down the hill toward the lake. When he reached the shore, he stretched his hands out and began to dance, grinning at the water just beginning to break through the ice, grinning at the sun. He looked as if he knew more about dying than anyone else did, than anyone else ever had, as if all death needed to be happy was a teddy bear and a dance.

Maybe he was right, I don't know. Merle was a lot smarter than he let himself on to be.

I walked down the hill to join Mom and Jackey. As we stood by the limo, people filed by us the same way they had filed past the casket in the church. The women cried and the men were solemn, and they all gave us hugs or shook our hands, but nobody would look us in the face. Not even Kelly. She hugged me long and hard, but she never looked me in the face.

"We can take the boys for a while, if you want us to," Gramma Tinsdale said. She and Grampa had flown up from Georgia. They both had tans.

"No." Mom shook her head. "The boys will stay with me. We'll be all right." Gramma hugged her. As she and Grampa walked away, George Shade took Mom's hand.

"I'm awfully sorry, Abby," he said. "I really am."

"Thank you."

"When you're feeling better, I'd like to stop by

and discuss something with you. Just call me when you're up to it."

She looked at him for a long time without saying anything. When she finally did, she lowered her eyes. "All right, George."

George walked away, but first he put his hand on Jackey's head, then mine. Even in the cool air, it was warm and wet. I didn't like the way it felt.

"Are you ready to go, Mrs. Morrell?" The funeral director held the limo's back door open. Mom looked at the mausoleum for a second, then nodded and stepped into the car. As I waited for her and Jackey to get in, I glanced over its hood. Ello Tohrey was talking to George.

"Joe didn't have to kill him," Ello said.

George shrugged. "What was he supposed to do? He didn't know who he was firing at."

"He still didn't have to kill him."

"You know how Joe is. Everyone does. Jack knew he'd be taking a chance stealing from him. He knew he'd be taking a chance stealing from any of us."

Ello looked at him. "Would you have shot him?"

"If I knew who he was?"

Ello nodded. George shrugged again.

"You're a bastard," Ello said. "He was our friend."

"Friends don't steal from friends." George wiped his mouth. "To be honest with you, I think Jack got what he deserved."

214

I waited for Ello to say something, but he didn't. I got in the limo. It drove us back to the church.

I don't know. It seems to me that you can never say anyone deserves anything.

It seems to me that if you didn't push a guy, you wouldn't have to.